Rick looked down at Star, and instantly she was mesmerized. Butterflies fluttered in her stomach. His gray-blue eyes scanned her face, and when he smiled she wished as hard as she could that she was four inches taller. She wished she had worn her peach-colored outfit, the one that put a glow in her cheeks and made her brown eyes even darker. The yellow sweat suit she was wearing made her look pale. And, oh, how Star wished she had put on a little makeup that morning.

"Can you make the photo shoot, Star?" Ms. Henry asked.

Rick's eyes were fixed on her. Star knew he'd be there and she knew she wanted to see him again. "I'll be there," she answered quietly.

Bantam Sweet Dreams Romances
Ask your bookseller for the books you have missed

Heart and Soul

Janice Boies

BANTAM BOOKS

TORONTO • NEW YORK • LONDON • SYDNEY • AUCKLAND

RL 6, IL age 11 and up

HEART AND SOUL
A Bantam Book / January 1988

*Sweet Dreams and its associated logo are registered trademarks of
Bantam Books, Inc. Registered in U.S. Patent and Trademark Office
and elsewhere.*

Cover photo by Pat Hill.

ISBN 0-553-26949-6

Published simultaneously in the United States and Canada

---

*Bantam Books are published by Bantam Books, Inc. Its trademark,
consisting of the words ''Bantam Books'' and the portrayal of
a rooster, is Registered in U.S. Patent and Trademark Office
and in other countries. Marca Registrada. Bantam Books, Inc.,
666 Fifth Avenue, New York, New York 10103.*

PRINTED IN THE UNITED STATES OF AMERICA

O   0 9 8 7 6 5 4 3 2 1

Heart and Soul

Chapter One

Star hummed quietly as she unzipped her yellow sweat jacket and entered the girl's locker room on Saturday morning. How could she have guessed twenty-four hours before that life would be so wonderful?

"Okay, Star Forrester, stop right there and start talking!"

The voice came from behind a row of lockers. Star peered around them and found her friend Liza wrapping a towel around her head like a turban.

"How did you know it was me?" Star asked.

"The humming. No other creature on earth makes a sound that horrible." Liza laughed. The girls often joked that Star's singing could make flowers wilt.

Star smiled. Since the night before she had been grinning like the Cheshire cat.

"Why didn't you tell me your dad's band would be in WWOW's top-ten Friday night countdown?" Liza demanded. "I tried calling you as soon as I heard the disc jockey announce it, but your line was busy for hours!"

"I wanted to call you, but every time my dad hung up the phone, it rang again!" Minutes after "I'll Never Have Another Love" had debuted at number eight in the countdown, Star's house had turned into a zoo. The phone had finally stopped ringing at about two in the morning, so it was no surprise that she had overslept this morning and showed up an hour late for swimming practice with Liza. "Hey, I'm sorry about being late. You've already finished your laps, haven't you?"

Liza waved off Star's apology. "Don't worry about it. No one else was here, either. Besides, it's the end of April; we won't have another meet for months, so it's no big deal. I'd rather know what it's like to hear your own father on the radio—on the top-ten!"

Star sat on the edge of the bench and dropped her gym bag on the floor. She tried to think of a way to describe the previous evening. So much had happened so quickly, and she wasn't sure where to start. "It was a total surprise," Star said finally.

"You're kidding! You didn't know the song was a hit until you heard it on the radio?" Liza reached for her sweater and tugged it over her head. "Did your dad know?"

"Yeah." A shiver snaked down Star's back as she recalled the scene the night before. "He made us sit in the living room—in silence. The only noise in the room was the radio. I was sure one of us was in deep trouble for something . . . until Dynamite Dave announced Blue Street Fog had the number eight song, and my dad's whole face just lit up . . ."

"I wish I could've been there," Liza said. "It must have been great."

"Better than great." Star nodded happily.

Liza took her blow dryer and started toward the mirrors. "So what did you do?" Liza called over her shoulder. "How did you feel?"

"I got all emotional and cried."

"That figures. What about Parry?" Liza switched on the blower.

"She kept shaking her head like it couldn't really be happening," Star said loudly so Liza could hear her over the noise of the hair dryer. Her older sister had tried not to cry, but Star noticed her eyes get shiny and wet.

"And your mom?" Liza shouted.

Star grinned. "My mom was great. She just rested her head against Dad's shoulder and looked at him with a dreamy smile. I could almost *feel* them both remembering the old days."

Liza snapped off the dryer, surprised. "Your mom—the practical one who always has her act together—was buying into your dad's dreams? She's too sensible for that."

"You can't call it a dream, not anymore. Not after last night. Blue Street Fog is back!" It came out louder than Star had intended.

"Pretty enthusiastic, aren't you?" Liza said in a dry voice.

"What do you expect from Jake Forrester's daughter?" Star said. Although she didn't remember the days when the band had been big—she was only a baby when they had had their last hit—Star had always shared her dad's belief that the band would hit the charts again.

"You know, you *are* just like your dad," Liza commented, flicking a comb through her short hair. "You both dream all the time."

"But look at all the terrific things that happen when you believe in your dreams." Star smiled just thinking about it. "The band is hot, and I had a good year on the swim team."

4

"Star, wishful thinking didn't turn you into the best freestyler on the team." Liza sounded tired of reminding Star of her own talents.

Star shook her head. "We're just sophomores. If I hadn't had my dreams, I wouldn't have had the guts to take on the older girls."

"Maybe." Liza didn't sound convinced. "So what's the next dream?"

"Well . . ." Star bit her lower lip, weighing the things she wanted most. Which one would she really concentrate on next? "It's being popular or growing four inches," she paused and then admitted, "or getting a boyfriend."

"A boyfriend?" Liza asked. "Do you have anyone special in mind?"

"No."

Liza leaned close. "Are you sure?"

"Positive. I've been so busy swimming that I don't even know any guys at Fielding."

"I know what you mean," Liza moaned, stuffing her swimsuit and towel into her bag. "We need to get around more."

Star grabbed her own gym bag from the floor. "What we need is a popularity project. If we can get into the right group, we'll meet lots of guys."

"Now you're making sense. Wouldn't it be great to have a whole group of friends?"

Pushing her lower lip into a pout, Star pretended to be insulted. "Thanks a lot. I thought I was your friend."

"You are." Liza hurried to explain. "You're the best, but wouldn't it be fun if we were both part of bigger group?"

"I know what you mean. Think of the parties." In her dreams, Star saw herself with tons of friends, staying out so late she wouldn't be able to get up Saturday mornings to swim laps. She and Liza had often laughed about being the only girls practicing early on Saturday, but it really wasn't funny. It only proved how boring their Friday nights had been.

"Parties would be okay. But what I'd really like is to walk up to a crowded table during lunch and have people move over to make room for me," Liza said.

Star could see Liza's point. Popularity meant more than parties; it meant belonging to a group.

"And go to the beach with them this summer," Liza added.

The locker-room door *swished* open, and the girls stepped into the school hall. "And play tennis," Star said.

"No." Liza's shoulders suddenly sagged. "Who are we kidding? It won't work. We're never going to be popular."

"Yes, we are." Star was firm. "If we want

this dream to come true, we've got to believe in it. I'm going to work on this, and we're going to be popular before school ends in June."

Liza grinned. "I'll trust you on the popularity thing, even though I'm still skeptical. But do you actually think dreaming will make you grow four inches?"

Star shrugged. "I can hope, can't I?"

She was tired of the way she looked. Her mom's word, "perky," described her perfectly. But she was tired of looking disgustingly healthy. She wanted glamour.

If she woke up one morning four inches taller but still the same weight, everything would be different. She would slick her hair back and wear big earrings. Choosing clothes would be easier because she could stop thinking about styles that balanced her broad shoulders. Her long legs would draw stares at the pool. She would look as if she were right off the pages of *Seventeen*.

Liza was thinking of more practical things than clothes. "It might mess up your stroke," she warned, as the girls started down the corridor.

"Don't worry," Star said with a laugh. "There's not much chance of my growing. It's not in my genes."

"I'm only thinking you should be careful what you wish for, because it just might come true."

Star barely heard Liza's last comment. At the end of the hall Ms. Henry, the girls' swimming coach, was talking to a boy. Maybe it was her anything's-possible mood that morning, or maybe it was fate, but Star's stomach did a flip when she looked at him.

The boy must have been nearly six feet tall, Star figured. His dark hair brushed his collar in the back. It didn't look styled, but it looked perfect. The best word Star could think of to describe his build was *lanky*; his long legs made him seem more slender than he probably was. He looked comfortable with his hands stuffed in the back pockets of his jeans. The camera around his neck swayed as he spoke. He grinned when he finished talking, and Ms. Henry laughed. Star didn't know why, but she couldn't tear her eyes away from him.

"Who's that guy?" she asked, feeling slightly irritated by her unexplainable attraction.

"I don't know," Liza answered. "Hey, are you taking this boyfriend stuff so seriously that you're going to chase the first one we see?"

"Like you said, you can't tell about wishes," Star said, but even she didn't believe wishes came true that quickly. Still, her mind was on the mystery man. They were close enough to hear what he was saying to their coach.

"Sure, Ms. Henry, I know it's a hassle, but you don't want this girls' team to be remembered forever as the one with an ink smear on their yearbook picture, do you?" His tone was teasing, but in a charming kind of way. His smile had a crooked tilt, and his eyes sparkled as he looked down at Ms. Henry.

"I can probably get the team together Monday morning right before school starts," the coach said. She turned and saw Star and Liza. "Hi, girls. Meet Rick Walsh. He's been telling me that the yearbook printer ruined our team photo so they need it retaken."

"Is there time?" Liza asked. "It's nearly the end of April."

"That's why we're going to shoot it Monday morning," Ms. Henry said. "Can you be there?"

"No problem," Liza answered quickly.

"How about you, Star?" the coach asked.

Star couldn't respond to the question. Rick looked down at her, and instantly she was mesmerized. Butterflies fluttered in her stomach. His gray-blue eyes scanned her face, and when he smiled she wished as hard as she could that she was four inches taller. And she wished she had worn her peach-colored outfit, the one that put a glow in her cheeks and made her brown eyes even darker. The yellow sweat suit she was wearing made her look pale. And, oh, how Star wished she had put on a little makeup that morning.

"Can you make it, Star?" Ms. Henry asked, repeating her question.

Rick's eyes were fixed on her, and Star knew she wanted to see him again even though she hated posing for pictures. "I'll be there," she answered quietly.

"Good. I have to call the rest of the team," the coach said, "I'll see you Monday morning at seven-thirty."

Ms. Henry walked into her office, with Rick at her heels.

"Are you all right?" Liza asked, waving a hand in front of Star's face. "You look like you're in a trance."

"He's not bad, huh?" she said, still staring after him. When Liza didn't answer, Star turned her attention to her friend. "Didn't you like him?"

"He's cute and all," Liza said. "But he was so busy looking at you that he didn't even see me."

Star smiled. "Do you really think so?" She had thought the same thing, but if Liza saw

10

it, too, then she knew it hadn't been her imagination.

"Yeah, I think so." Liza gave her a gentle nudge, and they started walking toward the double doors leading outside. "Do you mind if I come home with you for a few minutes? I'd like to see your dad and congratulate him on 'I'll Never Have Another Love.' "

" 'I'll Never Have Another Love'?" The question came from behind them, and Star turned to find Rick coming out of the coach's office. "Do you know one of the guys in Blue Street Fog or something?"

"Know them? She's related!" Liza exclaimed.

"No kidding?" Rick's eyes opened wide in recognition. "Your last name is Forrester, isn't it? You must be related to Jake or Gregg!"

Star smiled, surprised that Rick knew who she was. "That's right. Gregg's my uncle, and Jake's my dad."

"Jake Forrester's your dad? I knew you were Star Forrester, but I didn't—"

"How did you know my name?" Star interrupted with eager curiosity. Where had he been all year?

"I work on the yearbook, remember?" He shrugged as if he knew the names of every student at Fielding High, then continued. "I remember you from the swim season and all the records you broke in the freestyle races. But I never made the connection that you might be a Blue Street Fog Forrester. I mean, I'd heard Jake Forrester lived somewhere near Minneapolis, but I didn't know he lived right here in Fielding! Besides, I thought his kids had names like Garden of Eden or something."

Star's laughter stopped him. Finally catching her breath, she said, "You're thinking of my sister. Her name is Paradise, but if you plan to live long, you call her Parry."

"And Star's real name is Starshine," Liza said before Star could kick her.

"Starshine." He smiled. "I like that."

"How do you know about the band?" Star hadn't met many people her age who were interested in Blue Street Fog.

"I'm a fan."

"A fan? You're not old enough to know about the band. I mean, you're just a senior in high school." Most Blue Street Fog fans were closer to her parents' ages.

"I'm a junior," he said, correcting her. "But my dad saved the old BSF records. He still plays them all the time and I got hooked on them. And, I heard the new song on the radio last night. It was great!"

It was nice to talk to a real fan of her father's band, but at the moment Star was more interested in Rick. *He's a junior,* she thought. *Just right!* While a senior boy might be intimidating, a junior was only a year older than she was.

" 'A Lonely Evening' is my favorite BSF song. What's yours?" Rick asked, not seeming to notice she was lost in her own thoughts.

"My favorite?" Star muttered, coming back to her senses. "It has to be 'Welcome.' My dad wrote it the day I was born."

Rick's whistle split the air. "I don't believe it! I've never read that anywhere. Listen, do you need a ride home?"

Star felt Liza's eyes on her. Although she'd have loved to accept his offer, she couldn't disappoint her best friend. "Sorry, I've already got plans," she answered.

"No problem," he said. "Maybe I'll see you again sometime."

Star tried to keep her sudden smile under control. "You will—at seven-thirty on Monday."

Star and Liza bounded into the Forrester kitchen and dropped their gym bags on the floor. The house seemed quiet for a Saturday. "I'm home!" she called.

The girls heard footsteps hurrying toward the kitchen. Star smiled when her father came

13

into the room. He was wearing the "I'm a Rock Star" T-shirt that she and Parry had given him for Christmas. His hair was falling over his forehead and a faint stubble shadowed his chin. Star wondered if he was growing a beard to create a new image now that the band was back, or if he had just been too busy to shave.

"Hi, honey. Good morning, Liza. Are you two girls sure you want to be here? Everyone else rushed off when the *Rock City* reporters appeared on the doorstep at nine o'clock."

"Rock City?" Liza's mouth fell open.

"Yeah." Jake combed his fingers through his hair. "They're sitting in the next room."

Star pinched herself to make sure this was real. Copies of the trendiest rock magazine in the country could be found in every room of the Forrester house, but she couldn't believe real *Rock City* reporters were in her living room.

The phone rang and her father flinched. "Want me to get it?" Star asked.

"No. I can take care of it. Why don't you go on upstairs? There's no need for you to get involved in this circus."

He grabbed the phone as Star and Liza peeked into the living room to see the reporters before they hurried upstairs. It was an old house with the attic turned into a giant bedroom for Star and her sister. Liza made herself at home, turning on the radio and then sitting on the old sofa that was shoved against one wall.

Star sat cross-legged on her bed, scrunching a pillow in her arms. "Now let's get back to the most important thing that happened today," Star said with a mischievous grin. "What do you really think about Rick Walsh? Could he be a dream come true?"

Chapter Two

"There's Star Forrester. Isn't she lucky?"

"I wouldn't mind being in her shoes for a few days."

Star was surprised to hear a couple of people talking about her Monday morning as the swim team posed for the yearbook picture. The students were sitting on the bleachers by the pool, waiting for the photo session to be finished. They apparently didn't realize that their comments were loud enough to be heard. Star slouched, trying to hide. There was no way Rick could have avoided overhearing the topic of discussion in the stands.

"I can't see all the faces," he said, sounding official.

"What do you want us to do?" Ms. Henry asked.

"The people in the back need to stand taller. Especially the one in the middle—Star, is that you?"

The girls in the stands giggled, and Star felt her face heating up. Jenny, who stood on her right, elbowed her lightly in the ribs. Star straightened up quickly.

"That's better. Smile, ladies," Rick said. He must have clicked the camera a dozen times; all the while Star wished she could be anyplace but there. "That will do it."

The girls all heaved a huge sigh and hurried for the locker room. They had only fifteen minutes to dress and get to their first classes.

"That was rough," Liza whispered to Star.

"I felt like diving into the pool and hiding in the corner," Star said.

In the locker room Star's teammates offered their congratulations on her dad's hit song. Smiling, she accepted their comments. After all, she shared their excitement about Blue Street Fog's success. And the girls were just being nice—they weren't gossiping. Conversations quickly turned from Star to boyfriends and homework.

"Do you think people are going to bug you about your dad all day?" Liza asked. "If you want me to, I'll walk you to class."

"Like a bodyguard?" Star laughed. "No thanks. I don't want to make you late for class. I can walk alone. What could happen to me?"

Liza hurried out of the locker room while Star grabbed her books and purse. She was the last one to leave.

"There you are." Rick Walsh stood across the hall with his camera hanging around his neck.

"Hey, I'm sorry about the photo session," she said apologetically as he stepped toward her. Star was a little embarrassed by the scene beside the pool, but mostly she was pleased he had waited for her. "I hope all those people in the stands didn't distract you."

"Your fans?"

Fans? Why would *she* have fans? She looked up and saw laughter in his eyes. "I wouldn't call them that."

"Don't worry about them," he said easily.

"I guess they bothered me more than you." They started walking down the hall, and Star tried to ignore the other students whispering and pointing in her direction.

"I've taken pictures under worse conditions," Rick said, picking up the conversation.

"Yeah?" she said, challenging him. "Give me one example."

"The football team. They insisted on being photographed in gravity boots."

"You mean the things you wear to hang upside down?"

"That's right. And I had to wear the boots, too."

"You mean you were upside down when you took the picture?" He nodded and she laughed. "Why didn't you have the editor in charge supervise the shoot and straighten those guys out?"

"Because I was the editor in charge."

"You're the yearbook editor?" That was an important job, especially for a junior.

"I will be next year. This year I'm only the assistant editor in charge of all the teams and clubs."

"I'm impressed," she said honestly.

"Yeah?" He raised his right eyebrow. "And I thought I was doing it to get some practice as a photographer. I had no idea it would impress Starshine Forrester."

"Don't—" Her protest died on her lips. She was going to say, "Don't call me Starshine." Over the years, she must have heard every joke that could possibly be made about her name, and she much preferred to be called Star. But Starshine sounded special when he said it.

"Don't what?" he asked when she slowed down and stopped next to her classroom.

"I was going to ask you not to call me that."

"Starshine?" Her name sounded musical when he said it.

"Right." She smiled when a passing friend waved. "Normally I don't like people to call me that, but I guess I won't mind if you do— once in a while."

"That's good!" he said, flashing her an electrifying grin. "Look, I'd like to stay and talk, but I've got to get this film developed. I'll see you later." With a quick wave, he turned and headed around the corner.

It certainly had been an eventful morning so far, Star mused. At first she had thought the "fans" in the pool area would ruin her whole day. And then Rick had changed everything. Star couldn't help wondering how could a guy who took pictures while hanging from gravity boots find her exciting? She was just Star Forrester, a short sophomore swimmer.

Star paused in the hallway at the end of a long and tiring day and took a good look around. The normal end-of-the-day traffic had stalled around her locker. People didn't seem to be hurrying to catch buses, or meet friends.

Instead, they were standing around watching Star, and they weren't being terribly discreet about it.

"Hi, Star," a girl called in a nasal voice.

Star stood on her toes to see who it was. It looked like—no, it couldn't be. Star blinked and looked again.

"It's Sheila," the girl said loudly.

Sheila Stafford. Sheila, who had decided she couldn't talk to Star after her family moved into a house so large that they needed an intercom system to find one another. Sheila, who pretended she didn't know Star when they passed in the hall. Star was speechless.

Sheila wasn't. "I was thinking today that I really miss the old neighborhood. I was wondering if you'd mind if I came over to your house to see Parry and the rest of the family."

Like my dad? Star was catching on quickly. But she had nothing to do with Blue Street Fog's hit song. What did everyone want from her?

Star turned her back on them and whirled the dial on her locker. The door popped open, and she stashed the books she didn't need.

"What about it, Star? Can I walk home with you?"

Star wanted to scream. Sheila was waving her hand in the air like an obnoxious first-grader. Star turned back toward her locker and stared hard at the abstract design on her math book, hoping that by the time she turned around, they all would have disappeared. What more could happen that day? Maybe the *Rock City* reporter was lurking in the halls, too.

"Star? Are you in there?"

The voice was Rick's. Finally, there was someone she didn't mind seeing. "I'm here," she called to him in relief.

"I've been waiting for you. Did you forget our date?"

Date? He sounded so confident that it took her a moment to realize he was bluffing. But that didn't matter. What did matter was that he had offered her a chance to escape the crowd around her locker.

"How could I forget?" she answered, playing along with his game. "Excuse me," she said pointedly to Sheila.

Rick gently took her elbow and guided her through the crowd. When she felt his steady touch, Star realized she was shaking. She wondered whether she was reacting to the unwelcome attention at her locker or to the very welcome attention Rick was giving her. The flutter in her stomach told her it was Rick.

"Don't let them get to you," he said softly.

Star looked up and saw that the sparkle had left his eyes and was replaced now with concern. "I'm all right. I just didn't expect anything like this," she told him.

They stopped at the telephone in the school foyer, and Star dialed her home number. The busy signal buzzed in her ear, and she put the receiver back with a sigh. "I guess my dad's on the phone again. I really didn't want to walk home in the rain."

"I could drive you home," Rick said. "I brought my car today."

"I'd like that." Star didn't feel much like being alone after the scene at her locker. Maybe she should've taken Liza up on her offer to act as her bodyguard.

Star tried to settle into the passenger seat in Rick's car, knowing she should be relieved to be away from all the curious eyes at school. But it was so hard for her to believe what was happening that she couldn't relax. Would Rick have rescued anyone in her situation, or did he think she was someone special? Although Star couldn't be sure about his feelings, she knew she was definitely interested in him.

"Are you okay?" he asked, peering at her from the driver's seat.

"Sure." She looked around her and tried to act casual. "Nice car," she told him.

"It's nothing spectacular," he replied with a laugh. It was an old Mustang, but Star could tell he had kept it in good repair.

"As long as it runs, I'd say it's wonderful." Star really wanted a car of her own, but everyone at her house had given up certain luxuries in order to save money for her dad's band to cut their last album.

"It has a good sound system," Rick told her. He turned the key and the car jumped to life. The tape in the cassette player filled the car with sounds. Blue Street Fog.

"Not you, too!" she cried without thinking.

Immediately he popped the tape out of the slot. "I'm sorry. I was listening to it this morning, and I forgot it was in there."

"Don't apologize." Star stared at her lap, feeling like a fool. She wasn't talking to some kid hanging around her locker. This was Rick, the guy who had rescued her. "I overreacted."

He looked over his shoulder to back out of the parking space. "I haven't lied to you, Star. I am a BSF fan. If that bothers you, then I'll just drop you off at home and stop pestering you."

Star's breath caught in her throat. Just when she had decided it was time for a boyfriend, Rick Walsh appeared. It was too early to tell if he was one of her wishes come true;

still, the idea of not seeing him again made her hands turn cold and clammy. Star realized she felt good when they were together, and she didn't want that to stop.

She had to let him know his feelings about the band weren't a problem. "Hey, I can't hold it against you if you're a Blue Street Fog fan. I'm one, too." Looking at him, she grinned nervously.

"Good." He tossed her a smile before turning the car onto the street. "Where do you live?"

She gave him the address and then tried to explain how she had turned into a suspicious maniac that day. "You wouldn't believe the things that happened to me today."

"Try me."

"You saw part of it. People stared at me and whispered things in the halls and then all through classes. And my teachers were much nicer to me than usual. You know Mr. Mitchell, the biology teacher?"

Rick nodded. "My friends call him Mr. Pitch-All because he's thrown so many kids out of class."

"Even he was nice to me today."

"You mean he went all hour without yelling at you?"

"Better than that. When some of the kids

felt squeamish because we were dissecting frogs, he let *me* leave the room, but everyone else had to stay."

"Amazing. I had no idea it could be so useful to have a famous parent."

"If you think that was an advantage, wait until you hear what happened in the lunch line." She laughed, and it felt good to find some humor in her day.

The car slowed to a stop at a red light. Rick rested his arm on the back of the seat. There was a gleam in his eyes when he guessed. "They invited you to eat in the faculty dining room!"

"No. But it was *almost* that good," she said. "I have this absolutely crazy obsession for German chocolate cake. So today, when I got to the dessert section of the cafeteria line, I couldn't believe it—there it was—German chocolate cake! So the lady behind the counter says, 'Star Forrester, I just love the Blue Street Fog. When I was in college, I had their posters all over my dorm wall.' " Star mimicked the woman's voice. "And she gave me two pieces of cake!"

"You sure have it rough," he said teasingly as the light turned green.

"It's not all so wonderful. I mean, I couldn't

even call home for a ride because the phone's been ringing nonstop."

"At least I solved that problem," he reminded her.

She smiled and thanked him. Looking out the window, Star noticed the rain had turned to a mist and the sun was trying to peek through the clouds. She stared up at the sky and tried to think of something else to say. Her hand bumped the camera lying between their bucket seats.

"You seem to like photography." *Brilliant observation, Forrester,* she said to herself.

"I love it. You can capture some of the most amazing things on film."

"Like football players in gravity boots?" Star asked, expecting Rick to reply with a funny comment.

"No. That's just the stuff I do for the yearbook," he said seriously. "I'd like to be a photojournalist." When she said nothing, he tried to explain. "That's someone who takes pictures that have something to say."

She was confused. "What kind of things do they say?"

"Well, think of the photos in the newspaper that make you want to know what was happening when the picture was taken."

"You mean you want to hang out in war zones?"

"They don't have to be war reports. In fact, the pictures aren't always depressing." Rick paused as he glanced in the rearview mirror. "I could even shoot a roll of film around school that shows what it's like to live through a typical day of high school."

"That might be interesting. What would you do with it?"

"Well, I'd mount the best pictures and display them so that they told a story."

"Really?" She had never heard of anything like that.

"I don't usually bore people with this," Rick admitted. "It probably will never work out."

"Don't say that!" Star said firmly, and Rick looked at her, surprised, out of the corner of his eye. "Everyone should have dreams. Look where my dad's dreams have taken the band."

"I can't argue with that." He smiled. "So, what about you? Do you have dreams, Starshine?"

The question stopped her cold. She couldn't help squirming a bit as she clearly remembered listing her new goals for Liza: a boyfriend, popularity, and four inches. Star wasn't embarrassed by any of them, but she would rather die than confess to Rick that he was very possibly fulfilling one of her wishes. Although a cute answer about some outrageous plans might make him laugh and forget his question, dreams were too important to Star for her to turn the subject into a joke. She decided to tell him about one that had already come true. "Mostly, I've dreamed about making it as a swimmer."

"Are we talking Olympics here?" Rick turned the car down her street.

"No, I don't think so—" She could see her house in the middle of the block with people gathered in her front yard. Neighbors on both sides of the street were out on their steps watching the activity at Star's house. "What's going on?" she asked in surprise.

"Looks like a television crew," Rick told her as he parked his car behind a van that said News 13. He hopped out of the car and hurried to open her door.

He didn't need to rush. Star was having second thoughts about marching up to her house with the TV reporters there. She caught a glimpse of all three members of BSF standing together on the lawn.

Her father saw her in the car and waved.

"I can't believe it," Rick said half under his breath while he continued to hold the door.

"Want to meet the band?" she asked finally. How could she not introduce him? Until recently, she hadn't known anyone outside the family who seemed to care about Blue Street Fog.

Rick's eyes lit up. "Thanks!" He quickly helped her out of the bucket seat and slammed the car door behind her. By that time the news crew had discovered her, and a cameraman was recording their steps toward the Forrester house.

"Why is he doing that?" she whispered between her teeth. "I don't want to be on TV."

"Don't worry. They'll film fifteen or twenty minutes here and cut it down to three or four at the studio. We'll be edited out and left on the floor."

"Are you sure? How do you know so much about it?"

"I'm a photographer."

"What does that have to do with this?" Star asked, trying to ignore the camera.

She didn't have time to figure it out. A woman she recognized from the six o'clock news ran toward her with a microphone, and her father followed right behind.

"Do you live here?" the woman asked.

"This is my daughter, Star." Teasing, her father told the reporter, "She'll smile into the camera, but she doesn't give interviews—unless you want to talk about swimming."

He put his arm around her and brought her over to the band. She grinned at her uncle Gregg and Tucker Hart, the drummer. As usual, Tucker was the only one really playing up the rock star image with his leather vest and red headband.

"Who's your friend?" Tucker boomed.

Star grinned. "This is Rick Walsh. He helped me get out of school today."

"Was it that rough?" her uncle asked.

Star caught Rick's eye and knew he was thinking about the stories she had told him. But she didn't want to spoil the band's excitement by telling them about her disastrous day—especially since she knew they would blame themselves. "Let's just say it was different," she replied.

Rick shook hands with the members of the band and told them how much he liked their music. Then he tried to look cool when Tucker took him aside to discuss one of the band's early albums.

"We've got enough film here," the reporter announced loudly. "Come on crew," she said to the TV technicians. "If we hurry, we'll make the six o'clock show."

"Thanks for stopping by," Star's father said

sincerely, shaking hands with the reporter and her cameraman.

Star guessed her dad had found time to get ready for this interview. He was freshly shaven and he'd gotten a haircut. The new layered cut showed a little gray at his temples, but the white looked good in his dark brown hair. His deep blue eyes were alive with excitement.

"Do you like this publicity stuff?" she asked him as the news van pulled away from the curb.

"Sometimes I do. It helps the band," he explained. "We need to get the news out that Blue Street Fog is back. And all this publicity is the way to spread the word. But you don't need to worry about being chased by reporters, Star." His expression told Star that he understood how uncomfortable she was with the attention. "Let's go inside," he called to everyone left on the lawn.

As everyone else drifted indoors, Star found Rick shaking hands with Tucker and getting ready to leave. "You can come in, too. You don't have to go yet."

His gray-blue eyes were shining when he looked at her. "Star, I can't believe this. I never dreamed I'd meet BSF. But you've got a lot going on here, I don't want to intrude."

"I was starting to think we were friends,"

she said shyly, digging a hole in the lawn with the toe of her shoe.

"Yeah? I was thinking the same thing." He winked at her, and the teasing tone was back in his voice. "So maybe you'll invite me back sometime."

"Maybe I will." She looked up at him and tried to wink back, but she couldn't close one eye without closing the other and ended up making a ridiculously funny face. Rick laughed as he started to back away.

"I've really got to go. The swim team photo is in the car, and if I don't get it in the overnight mail, you're going to be in the yearbook with an ink spot right here." His fingers brushed across her nose. "I don't think you'd like that."

"Then hurry," she said with a smile. "I don't want ink on my nose."

"I'll be looking for you around school," Rick called out just before he ducked inside the car.

She hoped he would.

Chapter Three

Tuesday morning at school was quieter for Star. It seemed as if everyone had finished staring at her on Monday, and now Star was just another sophomore at Fielding High again. She couldn't have asked for anything better.

"Come on, I don't feel like sitting around in the cafeteria," Star said after she and Liza finished lunch. There had been no double dessert that day. Actually, one woman had tried to give her extra vegetables, but Star politely declined. She didn't like broccoli very much. "Let's go out to the commons." As the girls stepped outside into the courtyard that everyone called the commons, a gentle breeze ruffled their hair. Pulling her hands inside the sleeves of her sweater, Star glanced around.

Liza asked, "Have you seen Rick today?"

"Not yet." Star had called her best friend to fill her in on all the details as soon as he had left her house the day before.

"He sounds too good to be true." Liza shook her head slowly. "Maybe there really is something to your theories about dreams."

"I don't believe you just said that!" Star exclaimed.

Liza shrugged. "With evidence like Rick Walsh, how long can I keep disagreeing with you?"

Star nodded in agreement. Whenever she thought about the time she had spent with Rick so far, she felt warm and happy. There was definitely something special about him.

"Star Forrester!"

Star turned and noticed Cyndi Morris coming toward them, her blond bob bouncing as she walked. *The head cheerleader cannot possibly be talking to me*, Star told herself. *I wonder if there's another Star Forrester at Fielding High.*

"Hello, Star." Cyndi stopped directly in front of Liza and Star. "I saw you on the news last night. You looked great."

"Me?" The question squeaked past Star's lips. Of course, Cyndi was talking to her. After all, she *had* been seen on the six o'clock news with Jake Forrester's arm around her. Still, Star wondered why Cyndi Morris would make a special point to talk to her.

"Yes, you." Cyndi sounded friendly, and her smile was dazzling. "When I saw you on television last night, I asked myself if you were trying out for next year's cheerleading squad."

"Cheerleading?" Star knew she sounded like an idiot, but she still couldn't believe Cyndi was talking to her.

"Are you trying out?" Cyndi wrinkled her nose while she thought for a second. "I checked the list and didn't see your name. Did I miss it?"

"No. I'm not trying out for cheerleading."

"Why not?"

Liza shuffled her feet. Star knew her friend would like to have left, but she wanted to hear what else Cyndi had to say. "I'm a swimmer," she explained. "I don't have time for cheerleading."

"But you'd be great," Cyndi said, her blue eyes bright and sincere. "You're already athletic, and you'll be a junior next year, right?"

"Right."

"I definitely think you're varsity material!"

Star wanted to tell Cyndi Morris to get serious, but she didn't dare say that. Cyndi was a senior and very popular. Who was Star to tell her she was crazy?

"Then it's settled. You're trying out."

She could understand why Cyndi was captain of the squad. The girl seemed to have a talent for taking charge. Star didn't know where it came from, but she finally found the nerve to disagree. "I don't know. I haven't been to any of the practices."

"You have two weeks to learn the routines." Cyndi waved Star's concerns away with a flick of her wrist.

"Two weeks? I couldn't possibly be ready in two weeks."

"I'll help you myself," Cyndi said. "It'll be fun. And I think the squad could use someone like you."

Star looked at Liza who promptly rolled her eyes. Her friend wasn't offering her any help, and Cyndi was waiting for an answer. Finally Star shrugged. "I don't know what to say."

"No problem." Cyndi shook her head and her blond waves brushed her shoulders. "Take some time to think it over. I'll get back to you."

"Are you really considering it?" Liza hissed through her teeth after Cyndi bounced off to rejoin her friends.

"I know it's strange," Star admitted. "But this could be our big chance!"

"What are you talking about?"

"Popularity! Friends!" Couldn't Liza see the opportunities? "If I could be a cheerleader, then we'd have more friends than we can imagine."

"*You* would," Liza said, correcting her. "You'd be popular, and you'd have lots of friends."

"That's not—"

"Are things going better today?" Rick asked from behind them.

"Ask Star," Liza grumbled. "I have a math assignment."

Rick slipped in next to Star when her friend shuffled away. "What's wrong with her?"

"Cyndi Morris asked me to try out for cheerleading, and I guess Liza thinks it's a pretty stupid idea." It felt right talking her problems over with Rick.

"I didn't know you wanted to be a cheerleader," he said, sounding as surprised as she had been by Cyndi's request.

"I bet most girls think about it at least

once. I mean, it looks like a lot of fun. And cheerleaders are automatically popular—"

"With lots of boyfriends," Rick said, nudging her.

"That's not what I meant." She started to explain until she realized he was teasing her again.

"So, are you going to try out?"

"I don't know, but I'll have to decide soon. Cyndi's waiting for an answer."

"Let me know what you decide," he told her.

"Why?" She studied his handsome face. "Are you planning to show up with your camera during practice or something?"

He raised an eyebrow and tilted his head back. "You'll find out when it's time." He attempted a mischievous leer. "Are you worried?"

Star laughed. Worried? She couldn't wait to see what he would do next.

Star leaned on the counter at the Shirt Shop that night while her sister rearranged the T-shirts on the racks. The store wasn't glamorous, but Star felt comfortable there. A few years ago, when BSF had been at a low point, her dad had managed the store. Now

Parry was in charge and her long, straight blond hair swung from side to side as she worked. Parry had the extra four inches of height and slim body that Star wanted so badly.

"The shirts look fine," Star said from her comfortable position.

"I like changing the color groups," her sister said, tucking her hair behind her ears.

Star knew Parry was an artist at heart. She should have been in college that year studying fashion design, but she had decided to take over managing the family store for a while to help save money.

"Do you think you'll go away to school next fall now that the band is hot?" Star asked.

"It depends on how the album sells. One hit song isn't going to solve everything. They might have to cut another album before BSF is back where they want to be." Parry walked back and perched on the high stool behind the counter.

"I know," Star said.

Recording time in a studio was very expensive, and no one had been willing to invest in a band that hadn't had a hit for over ten years. Her family had saved for two years to collect their share of the money for recording the current album and the other band members had done the same.

"I just wish things could be different now that 'I'll Never Have Another Love' is up on the charts," Star said.

"Are you wishing for something else now, Star?" Liza called from the front door of the shop.

"Why should today be different from any other day?" Parry asked. "Of course she's wishing for something."

Liza walked into the store and leaned on the customer side of the counter. "Have you decided about cheerleading yet?"

Star felt Parry's curious eyes on her, and she could guess what her sister would say about cheerleading. But Star chose to ignore the early signs of tension in the air. "I've decided to do it. I'm going to try out for the squad."

"I don't believe you!" Liza exclaimed. "Think of all the time it will take. You won't have time for swimming, and the team needs you!"

Two women had wandered into the store, but they seemed more interested in the action at the counter than in the merchandise.

"Customers," Parry whispered, glaring at Star and her friend.

"But we have to talk!" Liza said insistently.

"Maybe you could do it somewhere else," Parry said, leaving her stool to assist the women.

"It's time for my break, anyway." Star walked around the counter and looked at Liza. "Let's go get a soda."

They got soft drinks from a hot dog stand in the mall and kept walking. "You've never said anything about wanting to be a cheerleader," Liza said thoughtfully.

"It does seem like a coincidence, doesn't it?" Star said. "I told you one of my new dreams was to be more popular. And now, I've got an opportunity I never imagined possible."

"I suppose you think your dream is coming true?" Liza didn't sound as if she believed Cyndi's offer had anything to do with Star's wish.

"Don't make fun of me," Star said defensively. "You know that all the good things I've accomplished have happened because I never stopped believing that my dreams would come true."

"There's nothing wrong with believing in yourself," Liza said. "More people should have faith in themselves. I just don't agree with you this time. Cheerleading isn't the answer to anything."

"But it's fate," Star said. "If someone's going to throw a chance for popularity in my lap, I'd be a fool to ignore it."

"Fate? Aren't you getting a little dramatic? We're only talking about cheerleaders." Liza slurped the last drops of soda from her paper cup.

"I don't know why you're so upset about this," Star said, honestly confused by Liza's attitude. "Think about all the friends we'll have when I'm a cheerleader. We'll be invited to lots of parties, and we'll sit at the best lunch table. We'll be busy all the time!"

"I bet!" Liza turned her back and started to walk away.

"Liza! What do you mean?"

Liza turned to look at Star with an unhappy face. "You'll be too busy with your cheerleading friends for me!"

Star walked back to the Shirt Shop alone, shocked by Liza's accusation. They were best friends. There was no way she would abandon Liza, no matter what. They were a pair, and they'd be popular together, she insisted to herself.

"You've got more company," Parry said as

Star stepped into the store. She pointed toward the racks in the back of the shop.

Star saw shining blond hair and realized that Cyndi had come to visit her. The giggles told her that Cyndi had brought a friend. Star smoothed her hair back and straightened her shirt. She took long, pointed strides toward the girls, pretending to be more confident than she really was.

"Hi, Cyndi."

Cyndi checked herself in the wall mirror and then turned. "Hi, Star. This is BJ."

"Hi, BJ." Star recognized the girl with curly red hair as another cheerleader.

"BJ's a junior and she'll be on the squad next year. In fact, she'll probably be captain, so I wanted you to meet her." Star raised an eyebrow in question, and Cyndi seemed flustered for just a second. "Oh, I'm sorry. I'm getting pushy. We came here to ask if you'd made a decision yet."

"Well, actually, I have decided to try out," Star answered quickly before either cheerleader could change her mind. Star didn't know why Cyndi wanted her, but she was not about to pass up the opportunity to improve her social life, and Liza's, too, of course.

Cyndi sighed in relief. "That's great. I was worried you might turn us down."

"When do I start learning the routines?" Star asked. Since she had taken them up on the offer, she knew she had a lot of work to do.

"We meet every day after school in the commons."

"Okay, I'll pack some shorts in the morning, and I'll be ready to start work tomorrow afternoon."

BJ gave Cyndi a meaningful glance, and Cyndi nodded. Examining Star's "Mondays Should Be Weekends" T-shirt, she whispered confidentially, "About practice clothes. Some of the girls wear old shirts and gym shorts, but that's not quite what we have in mind for the varsity squad. You'll do better with a matching outfit."

"Thanks." Star realized Cyndi must have really meant it when she promised to help, and Star appreciated the tip.

"Star!" her sister called impatiently from the cash register where she was swamped with customers.

"I've got to go," she told Cyndi and BJ. "But thanks for the advice. I'll see you tomorrow."

Star hurried to the counter.

The store finally quieted down by eight-thirty. Parry hopped onto her stool and let her head rest against the wall. "What a night. I almost gave the wrong change to two people before you finally came to help."

"Sorry about that," Star said wearily, leaning on the counter.

"What did those girls want? I've never seen them before."

"They were Cyndi and BJ from the cheerleading squad," Star explained, hoping Parry was too tired to get into it that night. She knew that her sister thought cheerleading was a waste of time.

"What's all this cheerleading business?" Parry didn't seem to sense Star's reluctance to discuss the topic—or she didn't care.

"They asked me to try out for next year's varsity squad."

Parry's mouth dropped open. "*They* asked you? Is there a shortage of girls trying out this year or something?"

"I don't think so." Star knew there wasn't. There had been at least thirty names on the sign-up sheet for tryouts.

"Then why did they ask you to try out?" Parry lifted her long hair to cool her neck and then let it drop over her shoulders again.

"I don't know." Star knew where Parry's

questions were leading, but she didn't know the answers. She was flattered by Cyndi's invitation and fully intended to live up to Cyndi's expectations.

"Aren't you curious? They must have a reason."

"Cyndi said the squad needs someone like me."

"And you believed her?" Parry shook her head at Star's apparent stupidity.

"Why shouldn't I believe her?" Star asked, knowing her sister would laugh if she told her the truth—that she didn't care *why* Cyndi wanted her on the squad. Parry would never agree that becoming a cheerleader was the solution to Star's not being popular. "Hey, don't spoil it for me. I know cheering wasn't your sort of thing in high school. You were into designing costumes for plays and artsy things like that, but you've never bugged me before just because I'm different from you."

Parry laughed. "We sure are different. I'm an artist and you're a jock. But cheerleading? It's fine for some girls, but it just isn't you, Star."

"That's your opinion." Star opened the cash drawer and took out the checks. With her back to Parry, she started listing them on the day's tally sheet.

Cheerleading might not fit Parry's idea of the old Star, but she had better be prepared for the new Star Forrester. Her name would be on the final roster when the squad was picked in two weeks. And next fall she and Liza would both be wrapped up in Fielding High's exclusive social scene. On impulse, she crossed her fingers and hoped Rick would be part of her new life, too.

Chapter Four

"Step, turn, step. Come on, Star, you can do it!" BJ was overcharged with enthusiasm, her red curls bobbing with the beat of the music.

"That's what you think," Star said under her breath as she tripped over her feet for the third time that afternoon. She hadn't realized the dance steps in the cheerleading routines would be so difficult. She *had* seemed to be catching on, but that day she was rusty. Sometimes Mondays were like that, she decided.

She looked at the other girls. They were having the same problems with the footwork. Liza had watched her second practice the week before and concluded that Star's body was much better suited to swimming. Star knew her friend wasn't being unkind. She knew she wasn't better than the other girls, but she wasn't any worse, either.

"Okay, ladies." Cyndi clapped her hands in front of the hot, tired cheerleading hopefuls. "Let's review the school song."

There were three rhyming verses to the song, and Star did her best to keep up with the routine. She could swim laps for half an hour and barely feel winded, but cheering practice was exhausting.

"Good work," Cyndi called from the front. "Take a break."

Star collapsed against a brick school wall on the edge of the commons and sank to the ground. She was replaying the last routine in her head, when a shadow fell across her face. Star looked up to see her swim coach. "Hi, Ms. Henry," she said from her position on the ground.

"Hello, Star. How's practice going?"

"All right," she answered, then added, "swimming's easier, though."

"I'd like to think you're a better swimmer than a cheerleader," the coach told her. "But I saw you practicing. You're looking good."

"Thanks." Star felt her face going pink.

"We'll miss you on the swim team," the coach said sadly.

"I'll miss the team, too." That was true. Through all the long, hard practices the girls had become friends. It would be strange the next winter not to be diving into the pool each morning before school for practice.

"Well, I wish you the best, whatever happens," Ms. Henry said before continuing across the commons.

Cyndi suddenly appeared at Star's side and squatted close to her. "I saw Ms. Henry talking to you. What did she want?"

"We were just talking about the swim team," Star said.

"Is she trying to convince you to give up cheerleading?" Cyndi's dazzling smile had turned into a worried frown.

Star was flattered that Cyndi was afraid Ms. Henry might talk her out of cheerleading. "Not exactly. She said the swim team would miss me."

"Will you miss them?" Cyndi asked, concern in her voice.

"Yeah."

Cyndi's face lit up. "I've got an idea. Some of the girls from the squad are coming over to my house tonight after supper. Why don't you join us? You'll like everyone when you get to know them, and maybe we can give you some tips."

"That would be great!" Star asked herself why Cyndi wanted to give her special help, but she had no answer, and she certainly wasn't going to turn down an invitation like that. Dreams were unpredictable. "Where do you live?"

The girls talked for a few minutes more, then Cyndi called the practice back to order. For another forty-five minutes Star stretched her muscles and gritted her teeth.

She pulled a towel from her gym bag and wiped her face as the practice broke up. She was relaxing with her face buried in white terry cloth when she heard Rick.

"Hey, Star."

"Tell me you haven't been watching me," she groaned from behind the towel. She was hot and tired—not exactly looking her best.

"Not for long." Rick caught the edge of the cloth and pulled it away from her face. He was grinning. "You looked even better than last week."

"That's good. I hope I've improved at least a little." She forgot how she must look because Rick made her feel comfortable.

He reached for her gym bag. "I've got a little work to do in the yearbook office. If you'll keep me company, I'll give you a ride home."

"You don't know how wonderful that sounds." Her feet were tired, and her muscles ached.

"I can guess," he answered, giving her a sympathetic look.

Rick recorded numbers on some order forms in the yearbook office while Star tried to relax at the worktable. Idly, she opened a file lying in front of her. It was full of black-and-white photographs. The first had been taken just as the place kicker on the football team missed the ball and fell on his behind. She remembered that game and giggled. The next picture caught BJ in the middle of a cheer. Her mouth was open so wide in the photo that Star could see her tonsils. Her giggles grew louder.

"What's so funny?" Rick asked from the corner.

"These pictures. Who took them?"

She was turning to the third photo when Rick scooped the file out of her hands. "I don't know who left this out," he muttered. His usually friendly eyes were dark.

"Hey, did I do something wrong?"

"Someone did, but it wasn't you." He dropped the file into the top drawer of the metal cabinet and then slammed it shut.

Star stood up, not sure what she should do. "Maybe I should leave."

He was at her side in an instant, his hand on her shoulder. "You don't have to go. I suppose I overreacted about those pictures, but they shouldn't be left out for everyone to see."

"Why, what are those pictures for?" It seemed as if Star had stumbled across something top secret.

"They're pictures that we took during the year that we decided not to use in the yearbook. They might embarrass someone."

"Like TV bloopers?"

"Kind of. We thought these pictures were too funny to throw away, so we saved them. It's kind of a joke with the yearbook staff, but no one else is supposed to see them."

"I won't tell anyone," she said, hoping it would help.

He tugged gently on her hair. "I know you won't. It's just that I feel responsible for yearbook things. If we decided the pictures were too embarrassing to be in the yearbook, then we're kind of defeating our purpose by leaving them lying around."

She saw his point, but she thought he was being too hard on himself. "I think you were being responsible when you put them away. Come on, let's get out of here."

"Good idea," he said, agreeing.

Rick's Mustang pulled into her driveway fifteen minutes later. When he came around to open the door, she smiled up at him. "You are coming in this time, aren't you?"

"I guess so," he said nervously.

"Follow me," she said. "No one will bite."

They went into the house through the back door and met Star's mother in the kitchen.

"Hi, Star. How was practice?" her mom asked, looking up from files she had scattered across the table.

"It was okay. Mom, This is Rick Walsh. He's the yearbook—"

"Oh, Rick Walsh," her mother interrupted, smiling at Rick. "Jake told me about you."

"He did?" Rick whispered, obviously flattered that a member of the Blue Street Fog would mention him to his wife.

"He said you helped Star out of some awkward situation."

"Mom," Star said, "I didn't tell Dad what happened last week. I didn't want to bother him."

"I know he doesn't know exactly what happened, but I bet I can guess," her mother said. "Everyone at school talked about you and made you terribly uncomfortable. People you barely remember suddenly wanted to be your friend again—"

It was amazing. Star looked up at Rick and saw he agreed. "How do you know all that?" she asked.

"Because all of that and more happened to me when I was dating your father and BSF's first song hit the air. I wanted to crawl under my bed and never come out."

Star had to laugh at the idea of her mother being frightened of anyone. "You obviously didn't do that."

"No. I kept going to my classes at the university, trying to ignore all the attention, determined to have a life of my own. BSF can have all the glory—I don't want it."

"Mom's the executive director of Time to Share now," Star told Rick proudly.

"The program that matches older people with day-care centers so they can act as part-time grandparents?" Rick asked. Star's mom nodded, pleased that Rick knew about her program. "I would love to get some photographs at one of the centers."

"You would?"

Her mother drew him over to the table, and he pulled out a chair. They huddled together over her calendar, and Star listened to them discussing an open house her mom was planning for July. She opened the oven door a crack. Tuna casserole. It wasn't her favorite, but she was hungry enough to eat anything. Practice had tired her out. She hoped she wouldn't have to do any more kicking or stretching at Cyndi's house that night.

"Excuse me," she said, jumping back into the conversation. "Mom, could I use your car tonight?"

"Sure, I'm not going anywhere. What do you have planned?"

"Cyndi Morris invited me to her house for some extra cheerleading help."

"That's nice." Her mom started to gather her notes and files in a stack. "You dad's been rehearsing today. He'll be home for dinner soon, so I'll finish these later. You're welcome to eat with us, Rick."

"Thanks, but I don't think I will," he replied.

"Don't you like tuna casserole?" Star teased him as her mother disappeared down the steps.

He pushed his chair back and stood. "What?"

"That's what we're having for dinner. If it's not the tuna, then why don't you want to stay for dinner?"

He looked down at the floor, embarrassed. "It probably sounds dumb, but this is all too much for me."

"My family is too much for you?" She lived with them every day, and she didn't see how they could be "too much" for anyone.

"You've got to see it from my point of view.

I've followed the Blue Street Fog for years, and it's a little weird actually talking to them like real people. I mean, your dad told your mom about me the way my dad might mention a guy my sister brought home. And now I find out you're so much like your mom. I mean, I read that your dad writes all of his songs about—"

"I'm like my mom?" Whenever she compared herself with her parents, she thought she was more like her father. They both had dreams.

"Of course," he answered. "Don't you know how much you look like her? You have the same shaped face, and your eyes tilt up the same way."

It was her turn to blush, and she felt herself going bright red.

"Relax," he said, teasing her, touching her hot cheek with a cool hand. "You look good to me."

Rick's touch caused another wave of heat to splash across her face. "Thanks," she replied.

Rick left then, before her father could show up and make him more nervous. Star stood in the door and waved. When he was safely out of sight, she whispered, "It's got to be him."

There was no question about it. Rick Walsh was the boyfriend she had wished for in the locker room. At first, she had liked how he looked and admired his confident, sometimes cocky, attitude. But now she had discovered sides to Rick that she enjoyed even more. She was pleased that they were both BSF fans. And she absolutely loved the way he turned shy around her family.

She always had fun with him, and more important, she felt comfortable with him. She smiled, remembering how understanding he had been when she exploded over the BSF tape in his car that first afternoon. And she had learned something else just that day in the yearbook office. When it came to something serious, he was responsible, someone to trust.

With Rick and cheerleading her life was really shaping up—better than she had ever imagined.

By the time Star arrived at Cyndi's house that night, there were already two cars in the driveway. Cyndi's mother directed her to the enormous family room where Cyndi and three other cheerleaders were talking.

"Come on down," Cyndi called to her.

Star straightened the pink top that matched the stripes on her white shorts. She had worn the outfit last week at practice and hoped no one would notice. All the cheerleaders seemed to have an endless supply of coordinated outfits, but Star's supply had just run out.

No one even looked at her clothes. They were too busy drooling over a magazine spread open on the floor. Star recognized the glossy pages as those of *Rock City* magazine.

"What do you think of Paul Gage?" Cyndi asked as everyone made room for Star in their huddle.

Star understood why the girls looked so dreamy. Paul Gage was the gorgeous lead singer in Dragon, the hottest rock group around. She thought he was dynamite, and obviously so did the cheerleaders. It was a nice surprise to discover they weren't so different from her. "I think he's terrific. Did you go to the Dragon concert last February?"

"We all went together and screamed ourselves hoarse," the little brunette named Bobbie told her.

"And I'm sure Paul looked right at me," claimed BJ. The others moaned as if BJ had told this story a hundred times.

"Did you go?" Cyndi asked Star.

"Yeah, it was great!

"I suppose your dad got you backstage passes," BJ said, sounding envious.

"Are you kidding?" Star couldn't think of anything more unlikely. Dragon was a hard rock band—not her dad's type of music at all. In fact, she thought he had never even heard of them.

"I guess it makes sense your dad isn't a Dragon fan," BJ said. The others nodded. "Our parents don't appreciate Paul Gage, either."

"But do you ever get passes?" Cyndi asked.

"Well, I never have before." Star paused, thinking for a moment. It would be fun to get passes to concerts. Maybe now that BSF was back in the top ten her dad would be able to get her some. "What if I could get passes for all of us?"

"Ooh!" Everyone loved the idea, and Star felt warm and happy. She and Liza had been right. It was going to be nice being part of a bigger group.

"Hey, guys," Cyndi said, getting more serious. "I told Star we'd help her with the cheerleading routines. All right?"

"Sure." Everyone nodded their heads in agreement.

"Some girls are having problems with their jumps. How are yours?" asked BJ.

"Not the best," Star answered.

"High isn't as important as neat," Bobbie said, advising her.

"That's right," said the one girl Star didn't know. She had been introduced as Tammy, and she was slightly rounder than the other girls. "Straight legs and pointed toes."

Star filed that information in the back of her brain. Maybe she wouldn't dazzle them with jumps that defied gravity, but she should be able to keep her legs straight and her toes pointed.

"Are your kicks okay?" Cyndi asked.

"They're about waist high."

Tammy whispered that her kicks weren't very high, either, and told Star not to worry about it. She couldn't believe how welcome the cheerleaders were making her feel. It would be worth all the work to be one of them.

Cyndi did a couple of kicks that were as high as her head. Without even breathing hard, she said, "I saw you leave practice with Rick Walsh today. Are things heavy between you two?"

Star was again surprised that Cyndi had been keeping such a close eye on her, and she didn't know quite what to say. "Actually, things are just getting started for us."

Cyndi walked over to Star and laid a friendly arm over her shoulder. "That's good. You're going to meet a lot of guys when you're a cheerleader. You might not want to be tied down so quickly."

"But I think Rick is nice," she said. It might be fun to meet more guys, but right then she liked being with Rick.

"He's okay," Cyndi said generously. "But he works on the yearbook, and he always has a camera hanging around his neck. Believe me, there are lots of great guys out there. Right, girls?"

With Cyndi's encouragement the others described their boyfriends. They sounded like great guys, but Rick still didn't look bad by comparison. And no matter what they thought, there was nothing wrong with having a camera around his neck.

"And you'll make lots of new friends. Everyone wants to know the cheerleaders," BJ said proudly.

As soon as she became a cheerleader and part of the popular group, the girls would get to know Rick and Liza, Star vowed. They would find out that Rick wasn't the nerd Cyndi seemed to think he was. And Liza would like these girls once she spent some time with them. Star had promised Liza they would be popular together, and it was so close to happening!

"What's wrong, Star?" Cyndi asked. "Are you worried about making new friends? Why don't you sit with us at lunch tomorrow and get to know more of the people we hang around with?"

Star wasn't worried at all, but she certainly wouldn't tell that to Cyndi and lose her chance to sit with the cheerleaders and all their friends. Even in her dreams, Star hadn't imagined receiving an invitation like this so soon. She hoped Liza wouldn't be mad about eating alone. After all, Star was doing this for both of them.

"Will you be there?" Cyndi asked hopefully.

"Sure." The next day would be another adventure for the new Star, but the old Star still had homework. "I might have to leave early, though. I've got a biology test right after lunch."

"No problem. We'll see you at our table," Cyndi said, smiling brightly.

Chapter Five

Conversations spun around Star as she sat at the cheerleader table during lunch the next day. They had been right about their boyfriends. Fielding High's cutest boys were sitting with them.

"So, tell us, Star, what's it like having Jake Forrester for a father? I mean, does he sing around the house and stuff?" asked BJ's gorgeous boyfriend, Kevin.

"He sings in the shower a lot," Star answered. Other times her dad hummed, especially when a new song was giving him trouble. "But the band hasn't rehearsed in the house since the time our neighbors called the police because they said the noise was disturbing them."

"And what about other rock stars?" Kevin asked then.

"Yeah!" The boy next to Tammy slid to the edge of his seat. He looked different from the other guys with his longer hair and a worn jean jacket. Star figured he was part of the group only because he had been the quarterback for Fielding High's district champion football team. His dark eyes were fastened on her face. "How often does Paul Gage drop by for dinner at your house?"

"Steve!" the girls cried in unison while Star covered her mouth to hold back a laugh.

"I'm serious," he declared. "Come on, Star. You must have met some other rock stars."

She shook her head. "No, I only know my dad and the guys in BSF," she said, sorry to disappoint him. But why did they expect her to know every act on MTV just because her dad was in a band?

The boy seemed to lose interest in her then until one more idea popped into his head. "If you meet anyone, you'll let me know?"

"Sure." Star had no problem making that promise. If she ever did meet a big rock star, she'd be more than happy to let everyone know.

"Hey, Cyndi. Are you getting ready for the carnival?" The question came from a big blond boy at the end of the table.

Cyndi narrowed her eyes. "Of course, we're ready."

"That's what you girls said last year," the boy said, pretending to cringe at Cyndi's glare.

"Nothing's going to happen this time," she said. She didn't bother to explain any of the details about the last year's carnival to Star. She must have assumed that they were common knowledge. "I've got plans."

BJ nodded enthusiastically to confirm Cyndi's announcement. "We're ready for anyone who thinks they can beat us."

Star was confused. She had heard about the year-end carnival at Fielding High. During the last week in May every year, all the school clubs worked together to organize a carnival, but she hadn't heard about any contest.

As she started to ask a question Cyndi looked around the table and asked in hushed tones, "Did everyone hear what happened in band today?"

The girls nodded and a few giggled, but some of the boys seemed interested in the latest bit of news. Star couldn't even begin to guess what had happened. Cyndi must have read the puzzled expressions on their faces because she hurried to explain.

"Renee Sharp told several girls that she's

absolutely positive that she'll make the cheerleading squad because her mother and my mother play golf together." Cyndi raised her eyebrows and waited to hear what the group thought of the situation.

"She's doing really well in practice," Tammy said.

"And she's a fox," Bobbie's boyfriend added. "Great legs."

"But she plays the trombone," BJ moaned.

"What bothers me is having people think we play favorites," Cyndi said. "Sure, her mom and mine are golf partners, but that doesn't mean Renee has an advantage over anyone else, like Star, for example."

Star felt uncomfortable in being drawn into the matter. It seemed as if they were going to decide right then and there whether or not Renee Sharp would make the squad. Although she was starting to feel like a part of the group, Star didn't feel right about listening to their discussion, especially since she hadn't even made the squad yet.

"If you'll excuse me," she said quickly, setting her empty milk carton on her lunch tray. "I have a biology test in my next class, and I need to study my notes some more."

Star gathered her books as some of the others in the group sighed and nodded understandingly. Star guessed that with their busy social lives, they did a lot of cramming. The cheerleading practice at Cyndi's house the night before had certainly messed up her schedule.

"Go ahead," said Cyndi, dismissing her sharply. She seemed anxious to get back to deciding Renee's fate.

As Star stood she saw a woman weaving her way through the tables. The lady raised her arm when she saw Star, and a stack of bracelets jangled around her wrist.

"Star Forrester?" she called. Heads turned at all the tables, and Star wanted to sink through the floor.

Star nodded and dropped back down into her seat. She realized immediately what the woman wanted. She didn't look threatening in her long, full skirt, leather boots, and stylish blouse. Her hair was very short, and it showed off her huge dangling earrings; gold chains fell around her neck in various lengths. She actually looked as if she might be very nice, but the notepad sticking out of her purse shrieked *reporter*, much to Star's dismay.

The woman extended her hand in Star's direction. "I'm Wendy Warren from *Heartbeat*. Could we talk for a few minutes?"

Star noticed Cyndi smoothing her hair when the woman mentioned the name of the weekly artsy newspaper in Minneapolis. "Have a seat,"

Cyndi said, motioning for the boy next to Star to move.

"No. Don't," Star said. In her mind she pictured her biology test with a big black F at the top, and she wondered how she could escape. Where was her dad when she really needed him? He knew how to take care of reporters.

"Star, I think it would be great if we talked to Ms. Warren," Cyndi said. The boy had scrambled to another seat, and Ms. Warren was making herself comfortable.

"I'm sorry," Star told the woman. She didn't want to make a social mistake that would put her next for discussion on Cyndi's target list. "I didn't mean to be rude, but I have to study for a test."

"Of course, if Star has to leave, I'm sure someone here would be happy to talk with you, Ms. Warren." Cyndi flashed one of her brightest smiles.

The woman cocked her head, and her chains shifted. "Thank you, but I'm here to talk to Star about Blue Street Fog." She turned her full attention on Star. "How do you feel about BSF's new hit? I bet you aren't old enough to remember the last one."

"But I've heard all the records," she answered with a self-conscious giggle. "I'm happy for my dad and the rest of the guys. They're finally getting what they deserve."

The woman smiled and started taking notes. Star hadn't meant to encourage her, but it was hard to keep quiet when someone asked reasonable questions about Blue Street Fog. But she still had to convince Ms. Warren that she didn't have time for an interview.

"It's great about my dad, but I still have to study for a test. My teachers haven't called off homework and tests just because my dad's in a band." She hoped the woman would get the hint that she didn't have time to talk.

"So being Jake Forrester's kid doesn't carry many perks around here?" the reporter asked, continuing to scribble notes. She obviously hadn't understood Star.

"Perks?" Star really hadn't done an interview before, but she had watched her dad often enough to know not to answer any question she didn't understand.

"Advantages. Like executives have company cars, and people working in stores get discounts. Isn't being Star Forrester paying off for you?"

"I guess not," Star answered after thinking for a minute. She thought about the extra cake she had received in the lunch line, but decided that wasn't important enough to mention.

"You're telling me your life hasn't changed?" Ms. Warren said in disbelief.

"Things really haven't changed," Star said. "I'm the same person I was before 'I'll Never Have Another Love' hit WWOW's chart. Now I really have to—"

"Study," the reporter finished for her. "Look, can we do more of this later today? My deadline is four o'clock."

Star sighed, wondering how to handle this problem without looking bad in front of the cheerleaders. Maybe Cyndi would be more understanding if she could make it sound as if she were doing the reporter a favor. "I don't have anything else to tell you. I'd hate to waste your time."

"There's plenty we can talk about. I want to know all about your dad," Ms. Warren said. "What's he like when he's writing music? Does he do anything unusual after a rough day with the band?"

Unusual? Ms. Warren wasn't the only one waiting for an answer to *that* question. The table was silent.

Star got the impression that everyone wanted her to say that dad tore the house apart or locked himself away in a temper when things weren't going well. She was tempted to tell everyone the truth—her dad would tinker at the piano as long as it took to solve a problem. His record so far was fifty hours—straight. It had nearly driven the rest of the family crazy. But that didn't sound like the kind of story Wendy Warren wanted for *Heartbeat*. Star didn't have any bad stories for Ms. Warren or the cheerleaders—and even if she had, she wouldn't give away her father's secrets.

"Sorry, I don't give interviews about my dad," Star said firmly. "You'll have to talk to him." She was stunned when she heard her own words. She sounded like some practiced movie star's kid who ran into the problem all the time.

Wendy Warren packed her notepad in her purse. "I'll do that. I've got an appointment with your father in an hour."

The reporter briskly made her way out of the cafeteria, ignoring the stares of the students. Star waved to Cyndi and the others and hurried into the hall through another door. She was glad she had a reason not to stick around the table to hear what they all had to say about the interview. And she certainly didn't want to run into Wendy Warren again.

Star headed for the library and noticed Rick walking a few feet in front of her. In spite of her biology test—the one that was going to ruin her grade point average—she wanted to see him. With Rick she didn't have to watch everything she said.

"Hey, Rick. Wait for me." She quickened her pace to catch up with him.

"Star?" He stopped and turned. "I looked for you during lunch. I saw Liza, but you weren't with her."

"I sat with the cheerleaders today," she told him.

"Ah—the big time." He fell into step beside her.

"Sometimes I think you're not impressed by the cheerleaders."

"They're all right, I guess." Rick didn't sound very convincing. "I've heard Cyndi is a loyal friend when she wants to be, but I've heard other things, too."

"What kind of things?" Star wasn't sure why she bothered to ask, since it was clear Cyndi considered her a friend. Why else would she be helping her so much?

"It doesn't matter," Rick said as they neared the library door. "You look happy and that's what counts."

"Happy? I've got a test in Mitchell's class in ten minutes. A test I'm going to bomb!"

"Sorry." He smiled at her and said quietly, "I was looking for you at lunch because I wanted to know if you'd like to go to a movie Friday night. Can you go?"

Suddenly Star heard Cyndi's voice in her mind, *"He's okay, but . . ."*

"I don't know," she said, "I'd like to, but—well, you know the way things are going lately. I'd better check at home first—"

What was she going to do? Star couldn't think of anything she wanted more than to go on a date with Rick, but she didn't want to risk any of the cheerleaders seeing them at the theater. Tryouts were next week and she knew she'd need Cyndi's approval. Although she had no intention of dropping Rick to please the cheerleaders, things would be easier if he had waited until after she made the squad before he asked her out.

Star couldn't believe the direction her own thoughts were taking. Rick was one of the best things that had ever happened to her. How could she wish he wasn't standing next to her right then, waiting for her answer? Dreams weren't supposed to be this complicated, Star told herself. She would have to do the only sensible thing—buy some time so she could figure it out later.

"I should have known," Rick said to himself, just loud enough so Star would hear it. "Of course, Star *Forrester* is busy Friday night. You're probably jetting to Los Angeles for a reception at a record company."

"Not you, too! This is me, Star. I don't know any rock stars. I don't fly across the country for dinner."

"You're going with me, then," he said, concluding logically.

"If I can," she told him sincerely. "I'll check with my parents tonight."

"Then I'll see you tomorrow."

"Okay." The satisfied smile on his face as he left her at the library made Star's stomach flutter. Things were going so well, maybe her luck would even last through the test.

When Star entered the library, she noticed Liza sitting at the first table near the door. Star knew her friend must be studying for the same test. She slipped into the chair across from Liza, wondering if ten minutes of cramming could possibly help.

"Are you ready for Mitchell's test?" she whispered.

There was surprise in Liza's eyes when she looked up, but the spark quickly disappeared. "I'm honored to be sitting with you, Star. It's too bad there aren't any cheerleaders in our class, isn't it?"

"Why?" Star had no idea what Liza meant.

Her friend slammed her book shut and pushed her chair back from the table. "So you could talk to them instead of me. I liked being your friend, Star. But it's not much fun being your friend only when the cheerleaders aren't around."

Star stared in shock as Liza stomped out of the library. She thought that Liza would have understood why she had been hanging around with the cheerleaders. They had stood in the locker room less than two weeks ago and talked about how they could get into the right group, and Star was doing her best to find a way for both of them. So why was Liza angry?

"Come over here," Cyndi called to Star after practice that afternoon, waving Star over to the circle of cheerleaders.

Star looked around the commons to make sure that Cyndi was addressing her. The other girls who hoped to make the squad were busy gathering their things together and rubbing their sore muscles. If they felt like Star did, they were so tired that all they wanted to do was go home and relax.

Cyndi motioned for her to sit down, so Star dropped to the ground in the spot the girls had saved for her between BJ and Bobbie. She surveyed the circle of girls. No one looked as exhausted as she felt.

"We were just talking about the carnival," Cyndi explained. "Do you know anything about it?"

"I heard about it when my sister went to school here," Star said. "I know the carnival is made up of clubs that all have booths."

"And all the money goes into the school activity fund," BJ said.

"This year the cheerleaders are going to make the most money," Cyndi said with authority.

"Do you keep all the money?" Star never realized that the clubs and teams had to pay for their own activities.

"I wish we did." Cyndi sighed. "But the money goes into one pile to be divided among all the groups."

"If we need more money during the year, we hold car washes and things like that," BJ told her.

"Remember how much fun we had last September?" Bobbie said. "The football team came with their cars, and they ended up splashing soap on everyone!"

"And think how many *more* people would come if we had a feature attraction." Cyndi put her hands on her knees and leaned forward.

"A feature attraction?" Tammy asked. "It sounds like you're planning to have a movie with the car wash."

"She means we could try to get someone to help us wash cars who would attract customers," BJ explained impatiently until Cyndi nudged her with an elbow. "I mean, we could try to get one of the players from the Minnesota Vikings or something."

"How are we going to do that?" Tammy persisted. Star wondered the same thing.

"Forget the car wash for now," Cyndi said in her businesslike voice. "Right now we need to talk about the carnival. We've been so busy with practice and tryouts that there are less than three weeks left for us to get ready. As most of us know, the cheerleaders always made the most money—until last year when the yearbook staff beat us." She wrinkled her nose at the idea of being beaten. "That's not going to happen again!"

"No way!"

"Go for it, Cyndi!"

Everyone agreed that the cheerleaders had to regain the top spot. Star felt honored to be included in the plans for the carnival. She wondered briefly why she had been invited to share in the discussion, when none of the other girls from tryouts were there, but she decided that Cyndi must already consider her part of the group.

"So, what's your plan?" Bobbie asked Cyndi.

"Just that everyone is going to work extra hard this year. No exceptions. Who wants to do what?"

Cyndi's question hung in the air for a moment.

"I'll work in the booth," BJ said, volunteering first.

"My dad can make the sign for our booth at his office," Bobbie said.

"And I can get flyers printed," Cyndi said. "Anyone else?"

Most of the others agreed to work in the booth after Cyndi promised to set up shifts so all the girls would have time to visit the other booths with their friends.

"My older brother is really handy with a hammer and nails. He can help us build the booth," Tammy said.

"Great." Cyndi clapped her hands. "What about you, Star?"

"Me?" Nothing could have startled her more. Star was just listening in on the discussion. "I'm not a cheerleader."

"Yet." Cyndi shook her head as if that was an unimportant detail. "Why wait until the last minute to get involved? Do you think your dad could help us on the booth?"

Star tried to imagine her dad with a hammer, helping Tammy's brother build the booth. She couldn't promise he would be much help, but he was always willing to help. "I think he will. I'll ask him."

"Super!" Cyndi was so enthusiastic that Star had to grin. "Now that that's all settled, it's time for us to get to work on our carnival assignments."

People started stretching and standing, and Star winced as she tried to straighten her legs. Her poor, tired muscles had stiffened in their bent position. Slowly, she stretched them out and tried to rub some feeling back into them.

"Have big plans for the weekend?" Cyndi asked, squatting beside Star.

"I might have a date Friday night," she confided. Star cringed inside, feeling disloyal for not mentioning Rick's name, but she had to be careful.

"You might? Either you do or you don't."

"I guess I do then," Star said as BJ came up on the other side.

"What would you say if we could get you a date with Mike Nelson?" BJ asked.

"Oh, sure." Star couldn't help laughing. Everyone knew Mike Nelson. He was a popular senior, gorgeous but a little wild. She doubted that he even knew who she was.

"Don't laugh," Cyndi told her. "I know he's looking for a date this weekend."

"For Friday night," BJ said specifically.

"Mike has a fancy new sports car," Cyndi added when Star hesitated.

"And I heard he's a great dancer." BJ's knowing look said Star would be crazy to pass up a date with him.

"Have you been out with him?" Star asked. Both girls shook their heads. "Then how do you know all this?"

"My boyfriend told me," BJ explained. "They're good friends. Are you interested?"

"I don't know."

"Come on, Star. You know who Mike Nelson is. We're talking major hunk." Cyndi sounded as if she'd like to date him if she weren't already involved with someone else.

"I still don't know." Visions of Rick kept popping into her head. He had been uncertain, almost nervous, when he asked her out that afternoon. But his usual confidence had returned in full when her excuses hadn't impressed him. Then he had flashed the devastating grin that drove Cyndi and the cheerleaders from her brain. How could she possibly consider hurting him by going out with Mike Nelson?

A nasty little voice inside her suggested Rick wouldn't have to know about the date. She could tell him she had some family thing scheduled for Friday. That was low, Star told herself, but she couldn't shake the thought. Guys like Mike Nelson just didn't ask out girls like Star Forrester. When would this ever happen again? She couldn't ignore the fact that this was a once in a lifetime chance.

If she could have one date with Mike Nelson—just to find out what it was like—then she could be Rick's girlfriend without always wondering what she had missed. Quickly, before she could chicken out, she said, "All right. It'll just be one date."

"Maybe two. He doesn't have a date for the senior prom yet, either," Cyndi whispered, giving Star a knowing look that said *It could be you.* "You won't be sorry," Cyndi said. Then she and BJ hurried off to start making the arrangements.

When the two girls were out of sight, Star sucked in a deep breath and then blew it out. Whether it was right or not, it looked as if she'd be Mike Nelson's date on Friday night. One date with Mike wasn't going to affect her relationship with Rick, she reasoned. And the senior prom wasn't really a possibility. After all, she and Rick hadn't promised not to see anyone else. They weren't serious. But if that were true, then why did she feel like a selfish rat?

Chapter Six

"Star, you're picking at your food," her mother said with obvious concern.

"Nervous about your date with Mike Nelson?" Parry asked sympathetically.

"Or guilty about not going out with Rick?" asked her dad.

"Honey! Don't be so hard on her," Star's mother came to her defense.

"I can't help it," Jake Forrester said insistently. "I was a teenage boy once. I remember how awful it was to ask a girl for a date, and I'd like to believe none of my girlfriends ever got a better offer and burned me this way."

"That's not fair," Parry said. "She never actually told Rick she would go to a movie with him tonight."

"That's right. We've both been teenage girls, and we know Star isn't breaking any rules. All she did was make a choice," her mother said, siding with Parry.

"Well, I hope for Star's sake she made the right choice," her father remarked. "I think Rick's a nice guy."

Star used her fork to paint her lettuce with thousand island dressing, trying to ignore the whole discussion. She appreciated her mom and sister coming to her defense, but it didn't help. Her dad was right. She hadn't felt too bad about telling Rick she had a non-existent baby-sitting job until he believed her. Realizing he trusted her, she felt like a creep for lying to him.

"Jake, you're not yourself this evening. Did something happen today you haven't told us about?" Star sighed in relief when her mother changed the topic.

"Are you asking me why I'm such a cranky old man tonight?" he asked.

"*I* wasn't going to put it that way," her mom said with a good-natured laugh.

Her dad ran his hands through the hair at his temples. "It's just been so crazy. Every time we turn around, there are reporters tailing us."

"We know," her mother said, and both girls nodded.

"You, too?" Her dad seemed surprised, as if his own life had been keeping him so busy that he hadn't realized they were being tailed by the media, too. "Do you know that Gregg and I had to *beg* some of these reporters for a little publicity in the past? Like Wendy Warren, the reporter from *Heartbeat*. We wanted her to come to one of our club gigs and write a story—just to let the world know that Blue Street Fog was still alive. Would she do it? No. But she was here this week, acting as if she had never met us before."

"Did you give her an interview?" her mom asked.

"I tried. Then Gregg and Tucker came over and started acting pretty weird. Tucker told her that he had joined a rock band just so he could meet women, and it was all downhill from there."

They all laughed. Even in the hardest times, Tucker had kept everyone smiling. When BSF could only get booked into small clubs, he had insisted the Rolling Stones would really love to play in an intimate setting like that, but they couldn't do it because their fans would tear the place apart.

"But not all the calls have been unwelcome,"

he said mysteriously. "Hugh Caster called me yesterday."

"From Caster Productions?" Her mother sounded really impressed. "What did he have to say?"

"He's putting together two national tours in the fall, and he wants to know if we're interested."

"Interested? Who would turn that down?" Parry asked, lifting her glass of seltzer.

"It's nothing definite," her dad said, hurrying to explain. "He's just making lists of groups who might be available to work with the big-name acts he's got scheduled."

"BSF wouldn't be the main act?" Star thought the man had called because people around the country wanted to see her dad's band. If they were the opening act, the audience probably wouldn't even bother to listen.

"Not yet," her dad said with a confident smile. "We need a few more hits. Caster doesn't think enough people would pay to hear the old music."

"That's not true!" Star said.

"Maybe not, but he's the guy with the money. Don't worry. If this isn't the year for a major tour of our own, it'll be next year."

"You and Star," Parry said, teasing them. "You're going to play Madison Square

Garden in New York, and she's going to be a cheerleader."

"How is the cheerleading going, Star?" her father asked.

"Fine. I'm learning all the routines and getting to know the other cheerleaders. They're really nice. In fact, they asked me to help with the carnival."

"That's quite an honor, isn't it?" her mother said.

"Actually, they asked if Dad could help with the booth." Star turned her expectant face to her father, hoping she didn't sound like just one more person who wanted a favor from him.

"What would I have to do? You know I'm not exactly handy—" His gaze drifted to the small dent in the wall where he had recently tried to stop a leak by the sink.

"Tammy's brother is a carpenter. I'm sure you'd just be helping him." Star was glad he sounded interested.

"Tell them I think I can hold nails for the guy or something."

Star breathed a sigh of relief. She didn't have to worry now. She could tell Cyndi that her dad was all ready to help out. "Thanks."

A horn tooted in the driveway, and Star

had the sinking feeling it was her date. After what her dad had said about Rick, she hoped Mike would come to the door so her dad could meet him.

Her dad raised one eyebrow. "Sounds like your date is here. Tell me, do you think Rick would be ringing the doorbell right now instead of honking for you?"

"You're right," Star mumbled. She pushed her chair away from the table and raced upstairs to brush her teeth. Then she ran to the door and hesitated.

"Good luck," her mom called.

"Same from me," Parry said.

It was usual for her mom to say that, but Parry didn't normally say anything. Her sister must think she would need some luck to get through the evening. Now that the big date was about to start, she wished she were going out with Rick. She never knew quite what to expect from him, but they always had fun. The horn blared again, and Star hurried outside.

Mike Nelson lounged in the car with his sunglasses low on his nose. His driver's seat was tilted so he could lie back and relax while he listened to the radio at full volume. He didn't seem to be in any burning hurry to meet her.

She opened the car door, and Mike glanced over at her as she slid into the passenger seat. He turned the radio volume down two notches and slid his shades low enough so he could peer over the frames at her. "Oh, hi. You must be Star."

"Hi, Mike," she said shyly, feeling very young suddenly.

They didn't talk much on their way to the party. He told her the host's name, but she didn't know the boy. Then he asked if her dad was really in Blue Street Fog. When she said yes, he just nodded. She tried to ask about his interests, but he turned up the sound on the radio and said he liked heavy rock.

She watched familiar landmarks pass by her window as they drove along. They followed her usual route to the mall, but then turned a block early. There was already a string of cars parked on the side of the road. Mike pulled into the first open spot and turned off the ignition.

Pointing to the new colonial house in the middle of the block, he said, "That's the place. His parents are in Hawaii, and we've got the place to ourselves."

Wonderful! Mike was taking her to an unchaperoned party. Her parents wouldn't be thrilled about that.

"Come on. We're missing all the fun." He had already hopped out of the car, and was now bending down to stare at her through the window.

It would be stupid to spend the whole night in the car, Star decided. Besides, Cyndi and BJ wouldn't have set her up with someone who was all that bad. She was probably overreacting.

"Let's go," she said, forcing a cheerful tone into her voice. She got out of the car and closed her door, expecting him to wait for her. When he didn't, she hurried across the lawn to catch up with him.

As they ran up the front steps a boy that Star had seen around school opened the door. "Glad you're here, Mike. Now the party can get started. Who's your date?"

"Star Forrester."

"The Blue Street Fog girl?" the boy asked.

"Yeah," Mike mumbled, tugging on her arm as he started down the steps to the party room.

She looked back over her shoulder and saw the boy shaking his head. She was getting used to people being surprised that Jake Forrester was her dad. Mike was one of the few people she had met lately who didn't seem impressed. Maybe he would be more interested if her dad were in a heavy metal band.

Heads turned as they reached the bottom of the staircase. In the dimly lit room, she couldn't tell if everyone was staring at her or Mike. Mike shoved his sunglasses to the top of his head and looked right at home, while Star knew she couldn't possibly look more out of place.

The girls at the party wore heavy makeup and clothes that were a little too wild for Star's taste. Star couldn't understand how these girls could feel comfortable in such tight jeans.

Star tried to ignore the tall blond girl who hovered around Mike. As soon as she had spotted him the girl hurried over to whisper something in Mike's ear, and he was still laughing in a low and rasping voice. The blonde threw one arm around his neck and kissed him. Wide-eyed, Star wondered why Mike had needed a date. He seemed to be enjoying himself without any attention from her.

"Mike?" Star touched his arm.

"Just a minute," he told her, holding the blonde's hand as she moved away.

This was embarrassing! Star pulled on his elbow. "Mike!"

"What, baby? You jealous?" His arms began to wrap around her, and she had to move quickly to slip out of his grasp.

Star hadn't been there more than two minutes, but she was more than ready to leave the party.

"Take me home."

Mike leaned close to get a good look at her. "Take you home?"

"Please."

"You don't mean that. You'll like it here once you meet a few people." He took her hand and started to walk farther into the room.

She wasn't going into any dark corner with this guy. And she wasn't going to stick around at a wild unchaperoned party just to see what might happen. Star stood her ground and refused to follow him.

He spun around when he noticed she wasn't moving. "What's wrong?"

"I want to go home—now." She said the words carefully and slowly so he would be sure to understand.

"Fine. Go if you want to, but I'm not leaving."

She yanked her hand out of his and raced

out of the house as fast she could. The fresh air was welcome, and she stopped to fill her lungs. The deep breath cleared her head, and then she realized she had no idea what to do next. She was too far from home to walk, and she hadn't brought any money to make a call from a pay phone.

She started walking, wondering how she had gotten herself into such a mess. Instead of having a nice, normal date with Rick she had chosen sleazy Mike. Why would Cyndi and BJ have done that to her?

She wanted to be angry with them, but she couldn't. Maybe they didn't know he was such a creep, Star told herself. Neither girl had dated him. Thinking back, she realized they had only told her what they had heard about him. Cyndi and BJ hadn't set up this disaster on purpose.

But she had to be more careful. Her wishes were coming true—when she became a cheerleader she and Liza would be popular. Mike Nelson had nothing to do with her plan. She had let Cyndi and BJ talk her into it. Star couldn't risk her dreams by allowing people to talk her into things she didn't want to do. The most important thing was for her to hold on to her dreams a little more tightly. She couldn't let anything happen that might spoil them.

Cyndi and BJ might be disappointed that she had blown her chance for a prom date, but they would understand. Her only real problem was Rick. It was going to be hard to pretend that her date with Mike Nelson had never happened.

Star stopped walking at a busy intersection to wait for a green light. She saw the mall just up ahead. What a relief. There was a phone at the Shirt Shop she could use! Feeling better, she headed for the store.

As Star entered the Shirt Shop, she heard two familiar voices. She stood quietly on the far side of a rack of shirts where she couldn't be seen.

"I think we might be able to help you," Parry was saying. "After all, it's for a good cause."

"So I can put the Shirt Shop down for a half a dozen shirts?" Rick asked, his pen poised over a clipboard cradled in his arm.

"I'll have to check with my dad. He owns the store, you know." Parry seemed to be enjoying her conversation with Rick, and Star wondered what they were talking about.

"Tell him the yearbook's raffle is an important money raiser at the carnival."

"You sure know your stuff," Parry said, teasing him.

"Laugh if you want to, Paradise Forrester, but that line got me a twenty-inch color TV set."

Star expected her sister to turn beet red and scream at Rick. No one called her Paradise. Instead, she flipped her hair over her shoulders and didn't seem to mind. "A TV? I'm sure. Bet you can't tell me who donated it."

Rick pretended to be insulted. "Don't you believe me? I got the television from General Electronics."

"They're on the other side of town. You're really taking this seriously." Parry actually sounded impressed.

"I've talked to someone from nearly every store in Fielding."

"And our store's at the end of your list?"

"Of course." Star recognized his tone and knew he was going to zing Parry with one of his lines. "I saved the best for last."

"Oh, get out of here, Rick Walsh. You'll get your lousy shirts, if you'll just leave me alone!"

When she picked up a shirt and pulled back her arm to pitch it at him, he ducked and tried to back out of the store. He didn't see the rack that was serving as Star's cover and he tripped over it. Shirts crashed to the ground as Rick rolled free.

"Star! What are you doing here? I thought you—" Parry caught herself before blurting out the news of Star's date with Mike.

"Star?" Rick turned and looked at her in surprise. "Didn't you have to baby-sit?"

"Not exactly," she muttered, starting to clean up the mess. As long as she concentrated on the shirts and the fallen rack, she wouldn't have to face Rick and admit that she had deceived him.

"You're not hurt are you, Rick?" Parry asked.

Rick shook his head. "Just embarrassed," he said, picking himself up off the floor.

"The insurance company won't care about that. But if you have whiplash or anything, you'll have to let me know so I can file a claim," said Parry, acting out her managerial role.

"I'm fine," Rick said, "but I'm sorry about the mess. Let me help you pick it all up."

"No, no. It'll be easier for us to do. We know where everything belongs. Why don't you just step out of the way?" With that settled, Parry started fussing with the merchandise. She bent down and whispered in Star's ear, "What happened to your date?"

"I don't want to talk about it," Star said, raising the rack back to a standing position.

Parry picked up some of the shirts on the

ground and smoothed them out on the hangers before putting them back on the rack. "I bet you don't want to talk about it because Rick might hear you. But you're not going to use me to hide from him. Now get out of here!"

Rick was still standing at the front of the store, and Star figured he was waiting for her. But what could she tell him? She spied Rick's clipboard down an aisle and saw her chance to talk to him about something besides her date.

She picked it up and walked over to him. "You don't want to lose your raffle records."

"No, I don't," he answered gruffly. He took the clipboard from her, being careful not to touch her hands or bump her arm.

She knew he was upset with her for her sudden appearance when she was supposedly baby-sitting, but Star had an idea. If she could keep him talking about the carnival, he might forget his questions. She knew it was a crazy plan, but she had to try.

"How are the raffle donations going? Are a lot of people contributing?"

Rick leaned back against the brick wall next to the Shirt Shop door, stuffed his hands in his jeans pockets, and looked right past Star.

She ignored the sinking feeling in her stomach and tried again. "Hey, I overheard you talking to Parry. If you're that persuasive with everyone, you must have collected a ton of things to be raffled—"

"Knock it off, Star!" he said. Suddenly his stare was locked on her, and his eyes looked angry. "Who cares about the raffle? Since you feel like chatting, why don't you explain why you lied to me?"

Lied. She wiped her clammy hands on her pants and tried to think clearly. Why had she believed one date with Mike Nelson wouldn't matter? Her plan to hide the date had never gotten off the ground. And now Rick was glaring at her, expecting her to offer some kind of excuse for her behavior. She didn't have one.

He coughed and shifted uncomfortably. When he finally spoke, his voice was flat, lacking its usual energy. "You didn't have to make up some story about being busy tonight. I would've understood if you said you just didn't want to go out with me. After all, you are Star Forrester."

"That not true!" she cried. "Being Star Forrester has nothing to do with us. I *wanted* to go out with you—"

She stopped as soon as she realized she had put her foot in her mouth.

"Now that's interesting," Rick said slowly. "What happened?"

Star figured she had two choices: She could tell him right then or tell him half an hour later after he had worn her down with questions. She took a deep breath and decided to save them both some time. "Cyndi and BJ set me up with someone else."

Rick's hands dug deeper into his pockets. His eyes were dark and there was a muscle twitching in his jaw. "Who?"

"Mike Nelson."

"Mike Nelson?" His voice was husky. "Where did he take you?"

Star didn't want to go into all the awful details. She wanted to keep her answers simple. "A party."

His eyes opened wide. "One of those big parties with tons of kids and music so loud you can't hear yourself think?"

"Yeah, something like that—I left immediately." She started to turn away, embarrassed by everything she had done, but she stopped when she saw a hint of a smile on Rick's lips. It wasn't a real grin, but the corners of his mouth were curved up just a little.

"You walked out on Mike Nelson?"

"Yeah." At least she had done one thing right. Now that Rick knew that, maybe there was a chance they could survive this disaster. His next question smothered her hopes.

"When were you going to tell me about this if I hadn't bumped into you tonight?"

"I hoped you'd never have to know." One look at Rick and Star knew he hadn't liked that. She tried to improve her explanation. "Well, it was just one date—"

"And you thought I wouldn't find out," he said, finishing for her, although she hadn't intended to be so blunt. She looked at the floor, unable to face him when he asked, "Is this supposed to make me feel better?"

Miserable, Star shook her head. She didn't know any way to make him feel better after what she had done.

"You're sounding and thinking just like Cyndi and BJ," he told her. "And I don't mean that as a compliment. Those girls do whatever they want and tell themselves that no one's going to be hurt. You're going to fit in very well when you're a cheerleader." He took a deep breath and slumped against the brick.

Star had no idea how to respond, but the sudden silence between them made her nervous. She had to say something. "I guess you'd rather not see me for a while." When he didn't disagree, she took a step back. "I have to go."

His arm shot forward and he caught her wrist. "Please, don't. We need to sort out a few things."

"Like what?" She looked up at him through her lashes. Was she insane for thinking he might still want to see her? He dropped her wrist and his hand disappeared back into his pocket. "I care about you, Star. My pride tells me to walk away, but I don't believe you normally do stupid, deceptive things like this. So what am I supposed to do with you?"

"I think you—"

"No, please." This time his smile was real. "You've done quite enough tonight. I need a few minutes to think."

Maybe he wanted to think, but Star would have preferred to escape the ideas spinning around in her brain. How could she have been so stupid? Sure, Rick was beginning to sound like he might forgive her, but she knew he could just as easily change his mind. She could still lose the best thing that had ever happened to her, and for what? She had wanted to know how it would feel to date a popular senior, and she had learned that Mike Nelson hadn't been worth it. If Rick would give her another chance, she would never hurt him again.

Suddenly he pushed away from the wall

and put his arm around her. He started walking and Star hurried to get her feet in gear. Where were they going?

"Did you really walk out on him?" he asked finally, an almost proud grin on his face.

"I sure did." Hope was rising again, and Star couldn't stop it this time.

"That does it, then. I can't help myself." The teasing tone in his voice was temporary. He turned serious and said, "Star, I just can't give up whatever it is that we have."

Forgetting the shoppers around them, Star threw her arms around his neck. Instead of stumbling from her unexpected attack, Rick stood his ground and hugged her back.

She was blinking back tears when she looked up at him. "I'm really sorry, Rick. What I did was stupid and mean. I'll never do it again."

He smiled down at her, loosening his hold. "Apologies are nice, but I want more from you, Starshine Forrester. Just how do you plan to make this up to me?"

Star stepped out of his arms and offered him her most charming smile. Could she have hoped for more? Rick was back to his outrageous teasing self. He had forgiven her! With an exaggerated shrug, she asked, "Exactly what would you like?"

He raised one eyebrow. "The movie you owe me. We can hold hands in the dark."

Star grabbed his arm before he could get away. She had been lucky not to lose Rick, and now she planned to hold on to him. Tugging on his sleeve, she asked, "What are you waiting for? Let's go!"

Chapter Seven

On the following Monday afternoon Star worried through her last practice before the tryouts the next day. She was convinced her kicks were too low and she would forget the fight-song routine. She would have been really depressed, but all the other girls sweating through the practice said the same things.

"Heard your date with Mike was a bomb," BJ said, standing with her hands on her hips while Star tried to perfect her jumps.

"It sure was," she replied breathlessly when she landed.

"Don't worry about it. Guess he wasn't your type, but there are plenty of guys around."

"I know a few guys myself." She and Rick had studied together the day before, and he had hinted that she should save the next weekend for him. Once they made up Friday night, they had both put her date with Mike behind them. Star knew better than to depend on BJ again. Rick would do her just fine from then on.

"Of course you know some boys," BJ said kindly. "But we thought you might like to celebrate this weekend with someone new."

"Celebrate what?"

"Making the squad," the cheerleader told her.

"Well, we can talk about *that* after we know if I made the squad." It seemed like bad luck to be too sure of herself, Star thought. Although she firmly believed in dreams, it was foolish to take things for granted.

"Does Chet Harper interest you?" BJ asked, catching Star's attention.

The football captain? How on earth would they set that up? Well, it didn't really matter, anyway. She would rather wait and see if Rick had plans.

"Look, if he's not good enough, we can find someone else—" BJ sounded truly confused that Star wasn't drooling over the idea of being Chet's date.

"Why don't we just wait and see how things

turn out," Star said, not wanting to push her luck the day before tryouts.

"Oh, I get it. You've got a bad case of nerves." BJ patted Star on the shoulder. "Don't worry too much."

Cyndi stood at the far end of the commons, clapping her hands. "That's it, girls. Practice is over. You all know the tryout procedure— group routines and then individual callbacks. Any questions?"

She waited for a few seconds, but no one raised a hand. Star wondered if everyone really understood the rules, or if they were worried about looking bad that late in the competition. Until the next day they would all be on their best behavior. A mistake this close to tryouts could spell disaster.

"We'll see you tomorrow!" Cyndi waved to everyone and wished good luck to the girls who stopped to talk with her for a minute.

Star had just flung her gym bag over her shoulder when Cyndi came toward her. "Ready to be a cheerleader?"

"I hope so," Star answered.

"And you'll be with us at the carnival won't you?" Cyndi asked.

"Sure."

"How about your dad?"

"He'll help, too." Star was proud that her

dad still had time for her between interviews and appearances.

Cyndi's face broke into a broad smile.

"The carnival really seems to be a big deal," Star said, chatting on. "I know Rick is busy getting contributions for the yearbook raffle. He even got someone to donate a television—"

"A television?" Tammy exclaimed from behind. "They're going to beat us again!"

"No way. We're going to be back on top again this year. Nobody's going to make more money than *we* do at our booth," Cyndi said, boasting.

"How can you be so sure?" Tammy asked shyly as if she were a little afraid to challenge the head cheerleader.

"It's guaranteed," Cyndi promised. "Every woman in town from fourteen to forty is going to line up at the kissing booth when they find out Jake Forrester is one of the kissers!"

Her father in a kissing booth! Star closed her eyes, wishing she hadn't heard that, but the words echoed in her head.

"You're not kidding," BJ said, joining the group. "I'm buying a whole roll of tickets for myself." She puckered her lips and the other girls giggled. Except Star.

"I thought you wanted him to help build the booth," Star mumbled nervously.

112

"Build the booth?" BJ hooted. "Why would we want him to do that? Do you think we would attract crowds by advertising that Jake Forrester helped *build* the booth?"

Star felt her face turning red, and the warm tingle in her eyes told her that tears were starting to pool. "Someone could have told me you wanted him for a kissing booth."

Cyndi's smooth voice replaced BJ's earlier rough tones. "The cheerleaders always have a kissing booth. Everyone knows that."

"I didn't," Star said.

Cyndi still tried to keep her voice soft. "You had to know, Star."

"I'm just a sophomore. I was in junior high last year, remember? How would I know about the cheerleaders' booth?"

"What did you think we do? Run a fish pond?" BJ inquired.

"Something like that," Star whispered, feeling dumber than she had during her biology test the week before.

"Well, Star"—Cyndi shrugged—"I'm sorry, but we can't help what you thought or didn't think. We've got a carnival booth to put together, and we sure appreciate you and your dad being such sports."

"Yeah. Sports." She bit her lower lip.

"Hey, you aren't mad, are you?" Cyndi

sounded surprised that Star wasn't going along with the deal.

Star swung her gym bag off her shoulder and held it in front of her body with both hands clinging to the handle. Mad? Hurt? A wreck? Star couldn't begin to define her feelings. She just wanted to get away from the cheerleaders and think for a while.

"I have to go. I'm late for work," she said as she hurried away. She didn't bother to look back—she knew the other girls would be talking about her.

"You're late," Parry called from behind the counter and then she took a look at Star's face. "Uh, oh."

"Don't ask me about it," Star snapped. She had walked for forty-five minutes and hadn't cooled down yet. How was she going to tell her dad that she had promised his services in a kissing booth?

"I don't have to ask you," Parry said with an unusual amount of sympathy in her voice. "I bet you've seen this."

Parry reached under the counter, and Star expected her sister to pull out a carnival flyer with a pair of red lips blazing over her father's name. Instead, Parry handed over the new issue of *Heartbeat*.

"I know you didn't say those things—"

Star's heart sank. Wasn't one disaster enough for Monday? What had she said to Wendy Warren that could make Parry's fair skin even paler than normal? While she stared dumbly at the newspaper, Parry turned to the center article.

"Blue Street Fog on Top Again"

Star skimmed the article, and nothing seemed to be too offensive. Ms. Warren made her dad sound like the boss. And Gregg sounded like a dedicated artist. He must not have done his John Wayne impression for her. And poor Tucker came off like a woman-crazed maniac. Apparently the woman hadn't caught on to his jokes.

"Jake's youngest daughter, Star, doesn't seem satisfied with her father's success. Rubbing elbows with Fielding High's beautiful people isn't enough for this petite social climber. When asked if she saw any advantage to being a Blue Street Fog progeny, her jaded reply was, "Things really haven't changed.' What did she expect? Three-hour lunches off campus?"

Star leaned across the counter, her head resting in her arms. She turned her face and her cheek touched the cool surface. Could she possibly pull a Rip Van Winkle and sleep for twenty years? People just might forget about this after that much time.

"It's okay," Parry whispered. "No one's going to believe you said those things."

Star stood straight and turned to her sister, her eyes wide with worry. "Sure they'll believe it. Liza already thinks I'm a snob. She'll probably paste the article to her bedroom mirror and read it every day for the rest of her life." Her eyes grew even wider. "And the cheerleaders? What if they see it? This could cost me a spot on the squad! They won't want a selfish social climber—"

"I don't know about that," Parry said, contradicting her and interrupting her self-pitying ramblings. "An experienced social snob might just be what they're looking for."

Star rested her cheek on her open palm. "Don't try to make me forget the article by making me mad. It won't work. I was already depressed before you handed me the paper!"

"You mean you hadn't seen it before?"

"No."

"Then why did you come in here looking like the world had just ended?"

"It hasn't ended yet, but it will very soon," Star said.

"Shhh—" Parry sounded like a tire with a slow leak. Star turned to look where her sister was pointing.

The man in the sunglasses and the Indiana Jones hat looked awfully familiar. A dimple dented his chin when he grinned.

"Dad! What are you doing in that disguise?" Parry asked a bit too loudly. He laid a finger across his lips to tell her to be quiet. More softly she asked, "Does this have something to do with your appearance on 'Twin Cities Happenings'?"

In the midst of her disasters, Star had forgotten the band had taped a local talk show that morning. It had been televised early that afternoon. She should have watched it, but then she would have missed practice.

"Did you tape the show on the VCR? Can we see it tonight?" Star asked, starting to forget her problems.

Her dad nodded, pulling off his glasses. "You should watch the tape. It would be terrible if you were the only two people in town who didn't see the show!"

"What do you mean?" Parry started to giggle.

"After Rick left the house, I came to do some shopping here at the—"

"Wait! Why did Rick come over?" Star couldn't imagine what Rick had been doing at her house. He had always seemed so shy around her family. And why had he stopped by when he knew she wouldn't be there?

"He just wanted to talk for a few minutes, and then I invited him to stay and watch the show with me."

"He watched 'Twin Cities Happenings' with you?" She felt a twinge of jealousy that Rick had watched the show with her dad instead of her, but then thought it was interesting that Rick had suddenly become so comfortable with her dad.

"Yeah. He's a nice boy."

"Never mind Rick," Parry said. "I want to know why you're doing this rotten Indiana Jones imitation."

"It's simple. I came to the mall right after the show and people recognized me. At first, they just stared. But then they started asking for autographs."

"I bet it was just like the old days," Parry said with a sigh.

"Hardly. In the old days, your mother didn't send me shopping for her when she couldn't get away from the office. I was in such a good mood, I even thought I'd surprise her with a present, but then I had women asking for my autograph in the perfume and makeup department!"

Both girls doubled over in laughter. Star knew her dad got embarrassed easily. He must have wanted to disappear in a puff of smoke when the ladies started calling his name!

"It's not funny," he said, protesting. "I bought the sunglasses and the hat at the boutique over there." He tilted his head in the direction of the Shirt Shop's neighbor. "I thought I would try them out on you. What do you think?"

"It might work," Star said.

"Maybe. I wasn't really sure it was you until you smiled. I couldn't miss the dimple," Parry said.

"Then it ought to work—unless my fans know about the dimple." He took off the hat and flicked a piece of lint off the crown. "What have you girls been doing?"

"Reading." Parry pointed to the article in *Heartbeat*. Star sometimes felt like putting a muzzle on her sister, and this was one of those times.

"Have you read it?" Star chewed her lower lip, waiting for her dad's answer.

"Yes." His voice was even. It didn't crack the way it did when he was upset.

"I'm sorry. I really didn't say what she said

I did." Her explanation sounded lame, even to herself. Who was going to believe it?

"Honey, I was very upset when I heard she had been to see you at school. There's no reason these reporters should be bothering you when you're supposed to be studying. Anyway, I got a little rude with Ms. Warren during my interview when she mentioned visiting you at lunch."

"I can see why you try to keep reporters away from us," Parry told him. "After that hatchet job on Star, I sure don't want to talk to anyone!"

"Not all reporters twist your words to make you look bad. In fact, sometimes Wendy Warren can be quite fair. But I think my comments about her interview with Star made her a little angry."

"So she decided to pay you back by making me look like the biggest jerk in Fielding?" Star was beginning to see she had been caught in the middle of something that had nothing to do with her. And she didn't like it one bit.

"I'm afraid that's the way it happened." He patted her on the back. "But people who know you won't believe the article."

"What about people who don't know me very well?" Like the cheerleaders? Did they know her well enough to see through the lies in the article?

"You can't worry about the whole world," her dad said consolingly. "You know the truth, and that's what's most important."

"I'll try to remember that," Star replied, attempting to convince herself that her father was right. After all, he must have gotten a few bad reviews in his time, and he had learned how to live with them.

He slid his sunglasses back on his face. "Well, I've got a little more shopping to do." He started to leave and then turned back to Star. "When am I supposed to help build that booth for the carnival?"

The carnival! Star had actually forgotten about the kissing booth for a few minutes. How could she tell him that he should forget the hammer and practice puckering? Her dad rarely even kissed her mom in public! He had worked so hard to protect his family's privacy, and she knew there was no way she could ask him to stand in the cheerleader's booth and kiss strangers.

"Star? Do you know when they're going to need me? The band has a lot of things coming up, and I want to work around this carnival deal."

She managed a smile. "Thanks, Dad. It was

really nice of you to make time for me, but Cyndi told me today that they have enough guys to help with the booth already. So you don't have to."

"Really? That's too bad. It sounded like fun." He adjusted his hat, tugging the front down to cover part of his forehead. "I've got to get back to my shopping. I'll see you ladies later."

"Why'd you do that to Dad?" Parry whispered angrily. "I think he was counting on doing this thing with you. He needs a break from all the band business. How could you tell him he wasn't needed? Were you embarrassed because he's so klutzy at fixing things?"

"Parry, you couldn't be more wrong!" Star said, exploding. "I did him a favor."

"Do you want to explain that?" Parry demanded, placing her hands on her narrow hips.

"Parry, did you know that the cheerleaders always have a kissing booth at the carnival?" Star asked, her face growing warm.

"A kissing booth? What does that have to do with anything?"

"A lot," Star snapped. "You must have known when you went to Fielding that the kissing booth is a tradition at the carnival.

You could have saved me a lot of trouble if you had told me."

"How would I know something like that? In case you've forgotten, I wasn't exactly the cheerleader type."

"I know," Star said with a sigh, her anger dissolving into worry. "I just wish someone could have warned me."

Parry was thoughtful for a minute and then she sucked in a deep breath. "Did they expect you to get Dad as one of the kissers?"

Star nodded her head miserably.

"How could you do that? You know how embarrassed Dad would be. Star, I can't believe you!" Now Parry sounded like a scolding older sister who knew everything.

"I didn't know what they wanted him for. They just asked if he would help with the booth, and I thought they meant help *build* it," Star said. "Then today Cyndi started talking about how much money they'll make when all the women in Fielding line up to kiss Dad!"

"That's lousy!" Parry exclaimed. "They've been using you. They asked you to be a cheerleader just so *Dad* could help them. How could you fall for that?"

"No. That's not true!" Star was adamant.

It was obvious now that Cyndi and BJ

weren't the most reliable friends in the world, but she simply could not believe what Parry said about them. They weren't exactly dependable as Liza had always been. Liza wouldn't have fixed her up with Mike Nelson. And Liza liked her dad a lot—too much to put him through an ordeal in a kissing booth. Suddenly Star had a lot of doubts popping into her mind. Had BJ known Mike was a jerk? Could Cyndi have purposely tricked her about the carnival? No! She didn't want to think that of her new friends. She knew that those things had all been misunderstandings.

She was so close to having it all for herself—and Liza. Star *did* have fun with the girls on the squad and she enjoyed being part of their group. Liza would feel the same way—she had to. She wanted to be a cheerleader so much. It was going to be great, and nothing could stop her now!

"Since you're determined to defend these girls, what do you plan to do next?" Parry clearly thought Star was making a big mistake.

"I've got to find a way to tell Cyndi that Dad won't be the star attraction at the carnival," Star said with a heavy sigh. "But I don't want her to be too mad at me—tryouts are tomorrow."

"Are you sure you still want to be a cheerleader?" Parry raised an eyebrow. "I mean, do you need their schemes and games when you're already on the swim team, and have good friends like Liza and Rick?"

"What can I tell you? Yes, I really want to find my name on the list of cheerleaders Wednesday morning. So what am I going to tell Cyndi?"

Parry smiled sadly. "That's your problem, little sister. Why don't you take the night off to think about it?"

Star's math book was lying open in front of her on the kitchen table, but she wasn't studying. For half an hour she had been rehearsing lines she could use on Cyndi—stories that would get her dad out of the kissing booth without upsetting her chances to be a cheerleader.

She could pretend her parents had suddenly remembered vacation plans for that weekend. Or, she could say Tucker Hart was getting married that night and her dad was going to be the best man. All she needed was a believable story.

"Would you like some company?" her mother's voice asked from the doorway.

"Not really." Star said without looking up.

125

"Even if I'm the company?" Rick stepped into the kitchen and Star's mom left.

"Oh, Rick! I didn't hear the doorbell. Did we have plans for tonight?" His right hand was behind his back. Was he hiding something?

"No, I just wanted to wish you luck for tomorrow's tryouts," he said.

She was touched by his thoughtfulness, but it didn't ease her worries much. "Thanks. I just hope it'll help."

Rick stepped closer to her. "Maybe this will help more."

His right hand came around and he handed her a single long-stemmed rose. She accepted it with a smile. "It's beautiful."

He pulled out a chair and sat next to her at the table. "Studying math?"

Star lifted the flower to her nose and breathed in the heady scent. Then she laid it across her open book. "It's no use trying to study tonight."

"You sound pretty low. Is there anything I can do for you?"

"Just seeing you helps a lot." She couldn't tell him about her real problem. Although he had forgiven her for the Mike Nelson date, he still blamed Cyndi and BJ for putting her in that situation. If she told him about the misunderstanding, she knew he'd say the same things Parry had.

"I know what's wrong," he said, sounding very sure of himself.

"You do?" Had everyone at Fielding High heard who would be appearing in the cheerleaders' booth?

"You're nervous about tryouts, but you don't need to be."

"Why not?"

"I've watched you practicing, Star. You're good." She blushed, and he said, "I just wonder what's going to happen when you make the squad. Are you going to have time for me, or will you trade me in for some football player?"

Star thought he was teasing until she saw real concern in his eyes.

She expected to hear that kind of thing from Liza, not Rick. BJ had already offered Star a chance at the football captain, and she had turned it down. Rick was the one she was crazy about. Being a cheerleader could never change that.

"Of course I'll still be with you. But what will happen if I don't make the squad tomorrow? Will you take a rose to some other girl who did?" she asked, teasing him.

"Don't even think that!" He leaned forward

in his chair, his face serious. "Cheerleading doesn't mean anything to me. I'll like you even if you don't make it, but that's not going to happen."

"I like your optimism," she told him. It was rubbing off on her. Star was convinced she would come up with a perfect story for Cyndi, and then she would surprise everyone with her dynamic tryout routines.

She couldn't help grinning. Her wishes were coming true, and it felt wonderful. She had a super boyfriend, and soon she and Liza would have the popularity they both wanted. Life just kept getting better all the time!

Chapter Eight

There she was. Star had been watching for Cyndi all morning, and now they stood facing each other in the hall between classes. Star's heart was pounding double time when she swallowed hard and called out, "Cyndi. Can we talk for a second?"

"Just a second," Cyndi said, waving to her friends who continued on without her. "With tryouts this afternoon, we don't want to make it look like we're too close," she said, flashing one of her prize smiles.

"Sure." Star hoped Cyndi would still be smiling after she delivered her news. "About my dad working at the kissing booth—"

"Yes? It's going to be great, don't you

129

think?" Cyndi looked past Star, smiling at more friends as they passed.

"Well, I just found out last night that the band agreed to play at a benefit in Seattle that weekend." Star couldn't look Cyndi in the eye as she quickly spit out the words.

"A benefit?" the cheerleader asked. Her smile had vanished, but she didn't seem *too* upset. "For what?"

"Uh—homeless children." Did Cyndi suspect it was a lie? Star wondered. Did she know Jake Forrester would probably be spending that Friday night watching a ball game or something on TV? Is that why she was asking questions about the benefit? Star held her breath and hoped Cyndi believed her story.

"We can hardly expect him to choose us over homeless children," Cyndi said reasonably.

"I really am sorry. I hope it's okay." Star smiled hopefully.

"It's not wonderful or anything, but there's not much we can do about it. Right?"

Star felt Cyndi's blue eyes focusing on her, and she willed her cheeks not to turn red. That would be a telltale sign. Trying to hide her nerves, she shrugged and told Cyndi, "I guess we just have to live with it."

"Sure thing. Hey, I've got to go before I'm

late for class." Cyndi turned and blended into the crowd.

Star wondered why she felt uncomfortable when she should be sighing with relief. She had gotten her dad out of the kissing booth, and Cyndi had stayed very calm. Maybe a little too calm. She hadn't said "goodbye" or "good luck."

Stop it, Forrester. Star had even more doubts then about Cyndi's friendship. Doubts were bad luck on tryout day. What she needed was a jolt of positive thinking. This was the day her dream would really begin to come true, she told herself. Why should she waste her energy on foolish worries? She resolved to concentrate positively on the tryouts. She'd really blow them away!

Star ran her fingers through her hair for the fifticth time, trying to keep her damp hair from sticking to her face. She knew her turn was coming up soon. It had to be; there were only three girls left for the individual auditions.

She hadn't done her best in the group routine. Nerves. No one had mentioned they would be using real pom-poms during the tryouts. All the fluff had distracted her, and the bright-colored streamers made it more obvious when her arm had gone up instead of going down.

Her strategy now was to dazzle the judges with her individual performance. Luckily, she had been near the back of the group when they did the fight song, so there was a chance the cheerleaders hadn't seen her mistakes. She rubbed her sweaty hands together and looked across the commons for some encouragement.

Rick caught her eye and winked. Although she figured he must have had a ton of raffle responsibilities, he had been watching the tryouts for the past hour. She forgot her nerves for a minute and mustered a smile for him. She wanted to let Rick know how much it meant to her that he was there.

"Is Star Forrester here?" Cyndi's voice rang in Star's ears, and she realized she had been daydreaming and almost missed her turn.

"Right here," she answered. Star stepped carefully around the other girls seated on the ground. A few whispered "good luck" as she passed. At that moment, however, Star was more concerned with trying to get some life into her legs. She had been sitting such a long time that her muscles had cooled. Even her fingers felt tense.

"Please hurry," Bobbie said.

Star moved to the center of the open spot in the middle of the commons. Without the safety of the group, she felt very much alone. There seemed to be over a hundred people lounging on the grass and makeshift bleachers, watching the auditions. From habit, Star tried to relax by shaking first one foot and then the other. It had always worked during swim meets.

"Let us know when you're ready," Cyndi called impatiently.

Star was surprised by the businesslike attitude of the cheerleaders. She missed the support she had become accustomed to receiving from these girls. Deciding to play it their way, Star brought her feet together and stood tall. "Ready."

"Please do the Touchdown cheer," Cyndi said. "Two sets."

Star cringed when she heard the choice. No cheer had more jumps in it than that one. How was she going to blow them away when her jumps were only one foot high? Gratefully, she remembered Tammy's hint that straight legs and pointed toes counted more than height. Taking a deep breath, she launched into the cheer.

"Down the field . . ." Star leapt into the air in a stag jump. With a smile, she landed solidly on both feet, then spun to the right to continue the cheer. Her voice rang out clearly and she knew her moves were precise. Finally, she prepared for the dreaded final spread-eagle jump. Gritting her teeth, she launched herself into the air, both legs out straight, her toes pointed so hard that they hurt.

Star landed neatly and felt herself go weak with relief. She hadn't gotten confused or made any mistakes. Star looked toward the cheerleaders, expecting to see approval, but no one even looked up from her score sheet.

"Let's hear Two Bits," Bobbie said. Glancing at the heap of pom-poms near the judging table, she added, "Use pom-poms for this one."

Star shook her head as she picked up a set of blue-and-white pom-poms. It was obvious they weren't playing favorites that day. She would really have to earn her way onto the squad.

"Two bits—" she shouted loudly and launched into the cheer with as much energy as she could muster. The cheer was a favorite of Star's and she felt her confidence soar.

"Four bits—"

She was moving perfectly with the beat, all the hours of practice were finally paying off.

The tension she had felt earlier was gone—for once her muscles were loose. She was actually enjoying herself.

Star took a deep breath and launched into the last set of kicks. Her right leg flew up past her shoulder, higher than it had ever gone. But as she brought it down Star felt the hamstring muscle straining. Determined not to let the pain show, she ended the cheer smiling. She was proud of her performance. She glanced in Rick's direction, and his wide grin sent a tickle down her back.

"Nice," Cyndi said, not sounding as impressed as Star had expected. "But could we hear it one more time, louder?"

Louder? She was so winded from jumping and kicking that her throat was burning. But if they wanted louder, that's what she would give them.

This time she concentrated on her voice, calling out the cheer with enthusiasm. She favored her right leg, so she wouldn't strain it any further.

She dropped her pom-poms in the heap when she was finished. She was breathing heavily as she walked back to the center of the open area and stood tall while the judges scribbled notes on their score sheets. She assumed they were checking her posture and smile. So she smiled.

"I think that's—" Cyndi was interrupted when Bobbie leaned close and whispered in her ear. Then Cyndi asked, "Could you do one more thing for us, Star?"

"Sure." When more of the judges huddled together, she wondered what they had in mind. Suddenly nervous again, she searched the crowd for Rick. Cyndi cleared her throat before Star could find him.

"We would like to see the Touchdown cheer once more—two sets."

The muscles in Star's legs screamed in rebellion before she even moved. It was going to be hard to do the jumps after the workout she had just given her body, especially now that she'd strained her right leg. But Star thought about the fun she was going to have when she made the squad, and how proud Rick would be to date a cheerleader, and how happy Liza would be with their instant popularity. Strained muscles were a small price to pay. She could always soak in a hot tub that night.

"Down the field . . ." she shouted, starting the cheer. She tried not to let it bother her that Cyndi and Bobbie talked through her whole routine, but it did give her an uneasy feeling. When she finished the second set, the judging table was silent.

"Thank you. Check the list in the morning," Cyndi finally said, dismissing her as she had all the other candidates.

Star stood there for a moment. She had expected something more; she wasn't sure what. But after all the time she had spent with Cyndi and the others, after all the encouragement they had given her, after the way she had just knocked herself out, why were they acting as if they didn't care?

When Cyndi looked past Star and called for the next candidate, Star quietly walked back to her spot in line. She didn't bother to watch the last two girls, and she only looked at Rick twice. Rick didn't know that she would have preferred to be alone, so he was waiting at the front door for her when she left the school.

"You looked really good," he said, complimenting her. He reached a friendly arm around her shoulder. "You'll definitely make the squad."

"I did my best." Star tried to sound confident, but she couldn't face him. Instead, she fussed with the zipper on her gym bag.

He took the bag out of her hands. "Something wrong?"

"Maybe it's just the letdown. You know, I've

been nervous about tryouts for two weeks. It's hard to know how to act now that they're over. Maybe I'm just worried about the list tomorrow." Half an hour ago she had been positive her name would be on the list. Why wasn't she so sure now?

"And maybe you're feeling betrayed by your new friends," Rick said, suggesting a possibility.

"Betrayed? What do you mean?"

"Cyndi and the others didn't seem to be too nice to you," he said, his usual teasing voice replaced by a gentle tone.

"What did you expect them to do? Leap from their chairs and hug me?" she asked, jumping unexpectedly to their defense. It had been fine for her to think something slightly strange had been happening, but it sounded ridiculous when Rick described it as betrayal. It sounded too much like the things Parry had said.

"Hey, relax." His arm was still around her and he squeezed her shoulder. "I just thought they would be more friendly."

Star had thought the same thing, but it seemed silly now. Cyndi had said just that morning that the cheerleaders couldn't act as if they were playing favorites. "If they'd been too nice, people would accuse them of being unfair."

"You believe that?" he asked doubtfully.

She considered it for a minute and shrugged. "I don't know anymore, but it doesn't matter. I did my best today, and now I just have to wait."

Star didn't look for Rick or Liza or anyone the next morning. She just hurried to check the list posted on the locker room door. There were only a few other girls there that early, so Star had a chance to look at the list closely.

When Star didn't see her name on the list at first glance, she started from the top and read slowly. She still couldn't find her name. She read the roster twice more, but there was no Star Forrester on the list.

She turned her attention to the junior varsity roster. After all, she'd be a junior next week. It wouldn't be so bad to wait a year to be on the varsity squad—even if she knew her individual cheers had been good enough to earn her a varsity spot this year.

When her name wasn't included on that list, either, Star backed away quietly. Her throat burned, and she knew tears would follow. The only thing for her to do was to head home and have a good cry. There was no way she could stay at school. She couldn't face Liza or Rick, not to mention Cyndi and all the cheerleaders.

"Did you see her staring at the rosters as if her name would magically appear if she waited long enough?"

Star recognized Bobbie's voice and flattened herself against the wall around the corner from where the girls were gathered.

"How dumb can you get? Did she really expect to make the squad when she didn't deliver her dad? There's no benefit for homeless children in Seattle." Star could hear BJ's know-it-all smirk in her voice.

"And Cyndi had hoped to get Blue Street Fog to sing at the talent show, too," Bobbie said.

"I know. She was sure the show would be a sellout, and she would be a hero for getting them to play. Boy, was she ever mad!"

Cyndi was mad? The day before that news would have made Star's knees shake. But after seeing the list, all Star could think was that she didn't care if Cyndi had been hurt, because Cyndi couldn't be hurting as badly as Star was right then.

BJ said smugly, "I even had plans to get the band to help with the car wash next year."

"Your plans went down along with Cyndi's,"

Bobbie said. "Who'd think a hunk like Jake Forrester would be stuck with a kid like Star?"

"Really." The voices were getting louder. Star began to move away from her hiding spot but not before BJ finished, "It hardly seems fair to the poor man."

Hurt and angry, Star ducked her head down and shuffled for the door. When she saw who was walking toward her, she bent her head lower and tried to push past him.

"Star!" Rick grabbed her arm and stopped her. "What's wrong? I was on my way to check the roster."

"Don't bother," she mumbled.

"Didn't you make the squad?" He sounded stunned.

Star closed her eyes to squeeze back her tears. Sadly, she shook her head to answer him.

He slid an arm around her shoulders and whispered, "Why not?"

"Because I wouldn't give them my dad for the kissing booth!" she said roughly. Her throat was burning.

"They wanted you to do what?"

The whole story came tumbling out. "They used me. They only wanted me on the squad so that my dad's band could help at car washes and talent shows. They never really liked me."

Star took a deep breath. "They were like everyone else who wanted to be my friend when BSF hit the charts, but they—I trusted them and they cheated me out of my dream!"

"I can't believe it," Rick said. "Who would ever figure that they'd try to use you just because of your dad's band?"

Just then a new truth jolted Star's muddled brain harder than a bolt of lightning would have. Who else did she know who thought Blue Street Fog was the hottest thing ever to happen in Fielding? Who else would have done *anything* to meet her dad? Who had been worried about losing her if she made the squad?

He was standing right next to her, putting on an almost convincing innocent act. She might have been stupid with the cheerleaders, but Star Forrester wasn't going to get burned twice in one morning.

"Get away from me," she said, backing away slowly. "You're no different. You're just like them."

Rick looked at her, puzzled. "What have I done? I don't understand."

He really puts on a great innocent act, Star thought. "You're no better than Cyndi and the others. You've only been nice to me so you could meet my dad and the guys in the band."

"Hey, that's not fair!" He jumped back as if he had been burned.

"Oh, no?" Her chin jutted forward. "You pretended to be shy so I would have to drag you home to introduce you to the band."

"I was trying to be considerate," he said, his thumbs hooked in his belt loops.

"Is that why you visited my dad when I wasn't home?" Now it made sense that he had dropped in to watch "Twin Cities Happenings" at her house. It was a chance for him to get to know her dad, and it had worked. Her father thought Rick was a nice guy!

"I wasn't visiting," he protested. "It was business."

"Sure. What were you doing? Getting autographs?"

He looked stunned for a few seconds. "Just forget that day, Star. You wouldn't believe me even if I told you the truth. But . . . what about your date with Mike Nelson?"

"Talk about not being fair!" Star was even more angry. "We agreed that was over."

"And it is," he said patiently. "Still, do you think it's easy for me, knowing you stood me up for another guy?"

She shook her head. He was making sense, but Star warned herself it was just an act. The cheerleaders may have lost their contact with Jake Forrester and BSF, but Rick was determined to keep his *in* with BSF. She was convinced he would say anything right then. "If Mike Nelson bothers you so much," Star said acidly, "why did we make up?"

He heaved a dramatic sigh. "Because I like you. I want to be with you."

"Just because I was dumb enough to believe Cyndi and the others, doesn't mean I'm stupid enough to fall for that line." Rick had swallowed his pride and taken her back for only one reason—he couldn't hang around the band if the two of them were no longer speaking to each other.

He raked his hand through his hair. "Look, as far as I can tell you're angry with me because I'm a Blue Street Fog fan. That's crazy—this whole argument is crazy." His arm stretched forward, begging her to listen to him. "You know we've got something special—"

"Save it," she snapped, unable to take any more of his lies, "for the next girl you meet whose dad is in a rock band."

"Okay," her father said, hanging up the

phone in the kitchen and coming to sit at the table with her. The wrinkles on his brow made him look worried. "What's wrong? You must have a good reason for coming home from school at nine o'clock in the morning."

"I didn't make cheerleading," she said, brushing the crumbs left on the tablecloth into a straight line.

"That's rough, baby, but don't you think your classes are a little more important than cheerleading?" Her dad leaned his elbows on the table, and it looked as if he were settling in for a long discussion.

"You don't understand," she told him before he could start his familiar routine about the value of school. "I found out they never even wanted me on the squad. They wanted you."

That piece of news made her father sit back in surprise. "Me? They wanted me on the squad?"

"Not cheerleading." Was he being dense on purpose? "They wanted you to be in their kissing booth at the carnival." His eyebrows arched. "And Cyndi wanted the band to play in some talent show. And BJ wanted you and the guys at her car wash."

"Maybe I should ask these girls to book some gigs for BSF," he said teasingly.

"Right. You don't need to sing at car washes in Fielding." The last thing she needed was a comedian.

"We might end up doing that," he said, suddenly serious. "Caster called this morning. He picked *younger* bands for the tours."

"Oh, Dad. I'm so sorry." Her personal disaster seemed to shrink in importance. Her father had been singing for more than twenty years, and she had been cheering for only two weeks.

"Don't look so sad," he said, making a face. "The band isn't really down to playing car washes. There will be other opportunities."

She wanted to smile, but this business had become too serious. There was something she had to tell him. "You know, Dad, maybe it's time we stopped counting on our dreams so much. All wishing does is set you up for being disappointed."

"Not you!" He looked positively wounded when he rocked back on his chair with his hand on his heart. "Your mother and Parry, and even Gregg and Tucker, have tried to convince me to quit dreaming. But you're my soul mate. We're both dreamers. Don't ever give them up."

"I don't want to believe in dreams and wishes anymore," Star declared. "You believed

146

in the band for ages, and I was so impressed when all those dreams took you back onto the charts."

"Just a minute, Starshine," he said softly, and she knew she was in for some fatherly advice. "The band didn't make the charts because I dreamed extra hard. We are where we are because we worked for it. Just like you dreamed about making the swim team, and then practiced such long hours that you almost grew gills. You won medals because you deserved them."

"And you hoped for a national tour," Star said bitterly. "You deserved it, but you didn't get it. I worked hard at cheerleading, and I really did well yesterday, but I didn't make the squad. If hard work doesn't make dreams come true, why bother?"

"Because dreams give us reasons to keep trying," he said simply. "Sure, I'm disappointed the tour fell through, but I honestly believe there are better things ahead for the band. And I know you still have dreams, even if you won't admit it."

She shook her head, but inside she knew he was right. What had she been looking for when all this business started? Ah, yes—popularity, a boyfriend, and four inches. The four inches were impossible unless she wanted to wear very high heels. And the boyfriend. She felt a pang of bitter disappointment when she realized how close she had come to having a boyfriend. Why did he turn out to be a phony. When it came to popularity, well, Star had bombed on her first attempt.

Unwillingly she did have to admit there might be ways to become popular without being a cheerleader. She had all summer to dream up a new plan of action. And that was a good thing, because right then all she wanted to do was crawl into her bed and forget that morning had ever happened.

Chapter Nine

"Rick called again this morning," her mother said at the breakfast table on Friday. "He wanted to know if you're going to school today."

"What did you tell him?" No one agreed with her new policy of refusing Rick's phone calls, but they all abided by her request, anyway. She didn't want to talk to him, yet she was curious about what he had to say for himself. So far, he hadn't offered any excuses or apologies.

"I told him you would probably be there." Her mom looked at Star's neatly pressed pants and top, and the blusher and mascara on her face. "It looks like I was right."

"Thanks for letting me stay home Wednesday and Thursday," Star told her parents sincerely. "I needed the time."

"No problem," her dad replied from behind his newspaper. Star hadn't realized he was paying any attention to the conversation. But when he continued, she wished he had been ignoring her. "I don't think you're being fair to Rick. He's worried about you."

"No," Star answered firmly. "He's worried about losing his contact in the Forrester house. For a BSF fan, he had a good thing going. You can't expect him to give that up without a fight."

"That's not true," Parry said, contradicting her from the hallway. "I can't believe he would use you that way." Star opened her mouth to argue, but Parry kept talking as she strolled into the kitchen. "Look, we're not all that gullible in this house. One of us would have seen through him if he was really taking advantage of you."

If they were so smart, why hadn't they warned her about the cheerleaders? Sure, Parry had said some nasty things about them, but Parry had never liked cheerleaders, so Star couldn't count on her to have an unbiased opinion.

"You just don't know how clever he is," she told her family, defending her stand.

She had fallen for his stories that first afternoon when he convinced her to accept a ride home. Rick had even managed to meet the band that same day. Talk about a fast mover!

What hurt the most, however, was that he had taken advantage of the Mike Nelson disaster. She had been ready to beg Rick to forgive her for lying to him. Little did she know that she was in no danger of losing him. She had felt guilty and she'd been scared to death when he uncovered the lie. And it had all been one giant waste of nervous energy. No matter how badly she embarrassed him, Rick Walsh would have stuck to her and Blue Street Fog like glue.

Her dad folded his newspaper and pushed back his chair. Standing, he looked down at Star. "Need a ride to school? The band's practicing for the River Fair," he said, mentioning a popular outdoor festival on the banks of the Mississippi River. "So I'm going your way."

"Blue Street Fog's going to be in the River Fair?" Star rose from the table, a broad grin on her face. "That's super, Dad! Why didn't you tell me before?" It wasn't as big as a national tour, but not every band in the Twin

Cities was invited to play at the River Fair with the name acts the promoter imported.

"Surprise." Her dad's grin was almost as wide as Star's. "See, dreams aren't so silly. You just have to be flexible."

"Dreams," Parry muttered, shaking her head.

"Don't knock it if you haven't tried it," her dad said with a wink.

"That's right." Star was beginning to let herself dream again as she prepared to rebuild her world. Her life hadn't been totally bad before she met Rick and discovered the cheerleaders. She decided she could survive if everything went back to the way it had been.

"I've got to go, Star." Jake picked up some keys from the counter. "Do you want a ride or not?"

"No thanks."

"If you're not ready yet, I can drop you off on my way to work," her mother said.

"Really, I don't need a ride," Star said. They were acting as if she had been terribly sick or something. "I have a date to walk to school with Liza."

"That's wonderful." Her mom had one of those smiles on her face that meant she was glad everything was going well with her family. "When did you two get back together?"

"We're not exactly best friends again—yet," Star said, trying to explain. "I called her late last night and we agreed we'd like to rescue our friendship."

"Good." Her dad grabbed an apple from the refrigerator and jangled his keys. "Liza's one of my favorites. I think she was the first person in Fielding to buy the new album."

There was a knock at the back door, and Liza walked in just as she always had in the old days, except that morning Liza was a little hesitant. She looked around the kitchen as if checking to see if anything had changed. Finally she looked at Star. "Ready to go?"

"Just let me get my lunch money," she answered, and they both started to laugh. It was an old joke between them. When they were younger, Star had so frequently forgotten her lunch money that Liza had gotten in the habit of reminding her every morning.

On the way to school Star gathered her nerve to talk about what had happened to their friendship. "I meant what I said last night on the phone. I'm really sorry cheerleading took so much time that I was too busy to be with you."

"I'm sorry, too." Liza didn't sound quite ready to forgive Star. "I felt awful when you always wanted to be with them. I had to eat lunch alone. I had to study alone. I even had to watch MTV alone."

"Okay, so I'm a rotten person. I'm trying to apologize." Star already knew she had been a disaster in the friend department, but Liza didn't have to make her feel worse.

"But how can I know you're really back? What if Cyndi decides she was wrong and works out a deal for you?"

"That's not going to happen," Star said with full authority. Even if she promised that her dad would work in kissing booths all summer long, Cyndi wouldn't take her back. She had embarrassed the head cheerleader, and she couldn't imagine many things that would make Cyndi hate her more.

Liza waved away Star's assurance. "Forget the facts. Just what if they asked you back? Or what if you were invited to be one of the Fielding Fifteen?"

Star could only laugh when Liza suggested that the school's elite singing ensemble might want her. The Fielding Fifteen won state awards every year, but they wouldn't have a chance if her voice were one of the fifteen.

"What's so funny? I'm only trying to make sure you won't abandon me again." Liza's lower lip extended in an exaggerated pout.

"Don't be upset," Star said quickly, realizing Liza really was insecure about their friendship. "But your choices are so funny. Can you imagine me in a singing group?" When Liza broke into a smile, Star decided she was on a roll. "My voice is so bad that my mother refuses to let me have a radio in the bathroom because the grout crumbles between the tiles when I sing in the shower."

Liza started to laugh. "I bet all the dogs on your block howl when you merely hum," she said, adding to the stories.

Liza's laughter was infectious. Star began to giggle. "You're right. All the singing talent in my family belongs to my dad. There wasn't any left for me."

After the giggles and laughter died down Liza had one more question to ask. "Okay, I believe you really want to be friends again. But I have to wonder why. Do you want me back just because you didn't make cheerleading?"

"You think I'm here with you because I'm hard up for company?" She had never thought of Liza as a last resort—they'd been friends for years.

"Something like that," Liza told her bluntly. "I can't help wondering if you would be walking to school with me today if you were a cheerleader."

"Just a minute." Star stopped in the center of the sidewalk. "You're the one who said you had to get to school early so we couldn't walk together anymore. I never said I didn't want to walk with you."

Liza's chin jutted forward. "You didn't have to say it. You were so wrapped up in your new friends that you didn't even miss me."

"Sure I missed you." Star was amazed that Liza really believed their friendship had ended. "Don't you know that I wanted both of us to be popular?"

"*Both* of us? What good would it do me if you were cheering while I sat alone in the stands at the football games next fall?" Liza started walking again.

Star hurried to catch up. "We both would have been more popular, Liza. Have you forgotten? We decided to make popularity our next goal."

"I still don't see how your being a cheerleader would make me popular. I'd believe you were joining the Fielding Fifteen before I'd buy that story," Liza said, scoffing.

"But it's true. Once I made the squad, I figured you would be able to spend time with me and the other girls, and we'd all be friends. Then we both would be invited to their parties and stuff."

Liza turned her head to stare at Star. Sadly, she shook her head. "I think all that dreaming has made your brain soft." Looking down at her muscular legs, she added, "Cyndi and her beautiful friends wouldn't want me around."

Star saw her friend's point. Now that she was thinking more clearly, she had to admit it was hard to imagine BJ and Bobbie shopping with Liza or talking about makeup techniques.

"So what was your real reason for trying out?" Liza asked as they turned up the school sidewalk.

Star had thought about that. Had it been for the popularity? Had she really wanted to cheer for Fielding High? Or had it just sounded neat to be a part of Cyndi's group?

"I really was thinking about both of us," she said. She had to make Liza understand that one of her main reasons had been their dream to be popular. "But I have to admit it was nice, feeling like a part of Cyndi Morris's group."

"I bet," Liza replied, but she didn't look angry any longer.

"But what's done is done," Star said with an ease that she didn't feel. No one except Rick and her family knew the real reason

Cyndi had wanted her on the cheerleading squad. It was just too hard to admit to anyone else that she had been used. She would let Liza believe she had simply not made the squad, and that she had come down with a deadly virus at nine o'clock Wednesday morning.

"Life will go on," Liza said wisely.

That was the biggest thing Star had discovered in the two days she had lounged around the house. She wasn't going to die because she hadn't made the squad. The sun would still rise every morning even if she weren't a cheerleader. She just wished she could feel that easy about a future without Rick.

She and Liza literally bumped into Ms. Henry at the door of the school. They were all trying to get through it at the same time.

"Star! How are you?" Ms. Henry asked. Her dark eyes looked worried. "I heard you were sick."

"I'm fine now," Star answered, looking at the floor. She hoped no one would ask for details of her dreadful illness.

"I'm sorry about the cheerleading results," the coach said as they moved into the commons. "But I can't say I'm *too* sorry. Now we'll have you back on the swim team."

"That's right." Star hadn't really thought through every consequence of the cheerleading fiasco. The idea of getting the kinks out of her body in the pool sounded good. "I'll have to get some laps in to make up for all the time I missed."

"Don't hurry it," Ms. Henry said cautiously. "Make sure you're well first." She paused. "But there is something you can do that isn't too strenuous."

"What's that?"

"We still have one shift open for the swim team's booth at the carnival next weekend. Could you help us out?"

"I'd love to," Star exclaimed. After all she had heard about the carnival, she didn't want to miss it. "Are you working, too?" she asked Liza.

"I hadn't been planning to," her friend said.

"Why don't you girls work together?" Ms. Henry said.

Star didn't want to speak for both of them. She wasn't sure that Liza was comfortable with their friendship yet. But when Liza looked at her with a big grin, Star knew it would be all right again.

"Let's do it!" Liza said, agreeing to the suggestion.

Star nodded, her smile just as wide as Liza's. "Thanks for asking us, Ms. Henry."

"I should be thanking you," the coach said. "You've solved my last carnival problem. Now I can relax."

Star joined Liza at their usual table during lunch. She had never noticed before how close their spot was to the cheerleaders' table. If she tried, Star could even overhear bits of their conversation.

She noticed several guys flirting with Renee Sharp. For some reason, Star couldn't help feeling as if Renee had taken her place. If Star had been willing to use her father's fame for a position on the squad, Renee would still be shining her trombone in the band room.

"Did you hear about Renee?" Liza whispered as if reading Star's mind.

"Hear what?" She doubted that Liza would know about Cyndi's mom and Renee's mom playing golf together.

"The day she made the squad, Mike Nelson asked her to the prom!"

So Renee even had Star's prom date. She was surprised to discover that although she felt a bit weird, there wasn't a shred of envy in her feelings. If dating Mike Nelson was required to make the squad, Star felt lucky that her name had been left off the list.

"Didn't you have a date with Mike?" Liza asked.

"You can't really call it a date," Star answered vaguely. "He's really a jerk."

Liza set down her hamburger, obviously more hungry for information about Star's date than she was for lunch. "Tell me about it!"

Star was so busy trying to think of a way to stall that she didn't notice Rick sliding into the empty seat on her other side.

"It's good to see you back," he said confidently, as if she hadn't told him get lost and refused all of his phone calls.

She looked over her shoulder and spoke through clenched teeth. "Go away."

He gently touched her arm, and she burned with anger. As if he could feel her temper, he pulled his hand away. "I really need to talk to you. I have to understand what's happening. I mean, I thought there was something special between us," he said quickly before she could stop him.

"You want to talk?" she said, turning to face him. "Answer one question for me."

He nodded.

"Would you have noticed me if Jake Forrester wasn't my dad?" She heard Liza's sharp intake of breath as they waited for Rick's answer.

"Maybe not, but it's a—"

She interrupted his excuses by turning her back on him and starting to stand. Listening to his lies wouldn't help her put her life back together.

Rick grabbed her arm, but her fierce glare did not stop him this time. He tugged on Star's arm until she dropped back into her seat.

"It's rude to ask a question and then walk away during the answer," he said evenly.

"And it's rude to take advantage of people," she replied, trying to slip her arm out of his grasp.

"I never took advantage of you." He sounded so innocent that Star wondered if he had any conscience at all.

"You don't call it taking advantage when you make friends with someone just because you want to meet her dad?" Her voice was icy.

"I wasn't doing that!" he said loudly, unable to control his temper any longer. He took a deep breath and tried to cool down.

"Quit lying," Star said in a soft but firm voice. "You just admitted you wouldn't have met me if Jake Forrester wasn't my dad!"

"It's a big school," he explained, finally letting go of her arm and running his hand through his hair. "There are lots of girls in this school I will never meet. I think I met you because you were on the swim team. You obviously prefer to assume I noticed you because your dad is in Blue Street Fog."

Star rubbed her forehead. "You're confusing me."

"Good." She made a face at him, and he wrinkled his nose back at her. "What do I have to do to convince you I like you for yourself?"

She had no idea. The day before it had been so clear that he had used her. Now he sounded truly concerned, and she wasn't so sure anymore.

He snapped his fingers. "I've got it. I'll help you make Cyndi and the others pay for what they did to you."

Star could see Liza paying close attention from the other side of the table. She knew her friend would eventually put the full story together. Hoping to keep the gory details from Liza at least a little while longer, she told Rick, "You really don't have to do that for me."

"I want to," he said, excitement rising in his voice. "Remember those pictures in the yearbook office? You only saw the one of BJ with her mouth open so wide you could see her tonsils. But I've also got one where Cyndi is kicking the wrong foot in a group routine. And I think there's a picture of Bobbie with her skirt flipped up too high. I'll get them and paste them on their lockers. That'll teach them they can't—"

"Please don't do that," Star said, begging him. Was this the same guy who had grabbed the file out of her hands so fast he had nearly given her a paper cut? What had happened to Mr. Responsibility? Had she driven him to this?

"Why not?" He leaned forward and peered into her face. "They ought to pay for what they did."

"Why?" Star just wanted to forget the whole thing had happened.

"Because everything was fine between us until they pulled this stupid stunt. It's their fault you don't trust me anymore."

"Wrong," she told him. "What's going on with us has nothing to do with the cheerleaders. They hurt me. And you hurt me. I just want all of you to leave me alone."

He must have heard the desperation in her voice because he shrugged and quietly got up and walked away without saying anything more. As soon as he was out of sight, Liza looked into Star's worried face.

"Star, what is *really* going on?"

Star bowed her head, hiding her face in her hands. She took a deep breath then lifted her head. "I'll tell you later, Liza, okay? Right now I need time. I have to get my quiet old life back together before I can talk about all the things that have happened to me recently."

Chapter Ten

"So Cyndi wanted your dad to be a celebrity kisser at the carnival tonight?"

"Shh—" Star hushed Liza as they both looked across the transformed commons toward the kissing booth. She had to stifle a giggle when BJ closed her eyes and puckered up for a greasy sophomore.

"Eight darts." A boy from Star's math class requested the darts as he pushed two quarters over the counter of the swim team booth.

Liza handed him the darts, and the girls moved to opposite sides of the booth while he took aim. His first three shots went wide, then he popped five balloons in a row.

"Very good," Star said, which earned a smile from the guy. She pulled a small mirror and a key chain from the baskets below the counter. "Which would you like?"

He pointed to the key chain, and he seemed to touch her hand unnecessarily as he took them from her.

"Uh-hum."

Star glanced behind the boy and noticed that Rick was next in line. He had cleared his throat to get her attention. Star felt trapped behind the counter, especially when her math classmate jumped and hurried off.

"You're scaring away the customers," Star said to Rick.

"Maybe Rick's a customer," Liza said cheerfully, making Star want to kick her.

Liza had been ready to personally strangle all of the cheerleaders when she finally learned the dirty details of their scheme, but her high opinion of Rick had never wavered. According to Liza, he was a victim and Star should take pity on him.

All week at school he had kept his distance, but he seemed to be everywhere she went. And since Star always hurried away, Rick never had a chance to talk to her. But that didn't stop him from grinning, winking, and making cute faces at her.

"Doesn't he look great tonight?" Liza whispered.

Star ignored her and tried to look past Rick, who had on a sports jacket with the sleeves pushed up to his elbows. A line had started to form behind him.

"Do you plan to play?" she inquired. "If you don't, please give someone else a chance."

"Give someone else a chance? Never. You'll always be my girl." He flashed her a wide grin that made her knees turn soft. "How much does this game cost?"

"Four darts for a quarter," she said impatiently. Every time she saw him, Star felt herself weakening. She hoped he wouldn't stick around the booth for long—he'd drive her crazy.

"What do I have to do?" Rick handed over a quarter. When Star wouldn't take it, Liza stretched out her hand.

"Shoot for the balloons," Liza said, pointing over her shoulder to the pegboard with the bobbing balloons. "If you pop more than three you get a prize."

"What do I have to do to win that?" Star and Liza followed his gaze to the large stuffed bear wired to the top of the pegboard.

"Break one hundred balloons," Liza laughed as she handed him the darts. "Think you can do it?"

"No problem," he said boastfully. "I'm going to win that bear for Star. How about it, Star?"

Star's patience was wearing thin, but the people in line didn't seem to mind. Apparently Rick was amusing them, but Star didn't want to be part of the entertainment, so she hid in a corner of the booth.

Two dollars later he still hadn't hit a single balloon. There was no longer a line behind him, but spectators had gathered to get a front row view of Rick Walsh making a fool of himself.

"So Star, when are we going out again?" he asked casually as he bent his right arm back in preparation for the throw. He brought the dart close to his ear and shut one eye to take aim.

The dart whizzed past Star, totally missing the board and sticking into the wooden frame. Star wondered if he might have done better with both eyes closed.

Rick shoved a dollar bill over the counter. "Sixteen more."

"Are you sure?" Liza asked, holding back his darts. "I think a lot of other people might like to try the game."

But the people gathered around the booth were obviously enjoying watching Rick and cheering him on.

"Sorry," Rick said, shrugging his shoulders. "I'll just have to keep shooting until I win the bear or Star agrees to talk to me."

Star didn't need to hear what Liza had to say; her friend's pleading eyes said it all. Liza spoke anyway. "Be a sport. Talk to the guy."

"I have nothing to say to him," she said firmly.

Rick reached out for the darts, but Liza put them behind her back. "Star! This is turning into a circus. Our shift is almost over and I can cover things here. Go talk to him alone—without an audience."

Liza made one good point in Star's opinion. Rick seemed determined to discuss their problem, and if she didn't stop him soon, he would do it in front of the whole school! His dollar bill still lay on the counter, so Star handed it back to him. "Keep your money. I'll listen for five minutes."

Star heard people clapping and whistling as Liza lifted one section of the counter and she ducked under it. Rick took Star's hand in his before she had time to object.

"I've missed you," he whispered as they lost themselves in the mass of people wandering from booth to booth.

She wished she could say the same thing. Sure, she had missed the boy she used to think of as Rick. Who wouldn't? Before she found out the truth, Rick had seemed like the perfect boyfriend. Star told herself to be careful. The real Rick and the phony Rick both held hands the same way, and his warm touch was tempting her to forget what she had learned about him.

"Liza said you needed time to get your life back together." His eyes were twinkling when he asked, "Has one week been long enough?"

To completely rebuild her dreams? He couldn't be serious. Still, each day was getting a little easier.

"Well, I have stopped hiding in the restrooms every time I see a cheerleader," she told him. Star refused to add how much longer it would take before she didn't hurt every time she saw him.

Rick stopped walking and turned her to face him, placing a hand on each of her shoulders. "Promise me one thing. Don't make your life exactly the way it was before BSF made WWOW's countdown—save room for me."

She bit her lip, reminding herself that there were many reasons not to trust him. "I don't think so," she said halfheartedly.

"You aren't listening to me. I'm telling you that I've been unfairly accused of using you. It's simply not true."

She looked up at him, wishing with all her heart that she could believe him.

He bent forward and dropped an unexpected kiss on her forehead. "I wish I could prove my innocence, Star, but there's no way I can do that. You'll have to trust me."

The quiet sincerity in his voice made Star wonder if she had been totally wrong about Rick. It was a frightening thought.

With one hand he brushed back a strand of hair that had fallen onto her face. "I can see I'm not getting very far with you. Maybe we should start over? I met you just when you became a hot item around Fielding. Our timing couldn't have been worse."

Star raised a hand to her temple, trying to slow her spinning thoughts. "Starting over won't help unless we settle this thing about my dad first."

"Okay!" His face lit up with enthusiasm. "Let's settle it right now. I'm a real fan of six bands. And I cannot claim that I haven't fantasized meeting them, but"—he crossed his heart with his right hand—"it's honestly a coincidence that I met you and liked you, and then your dad turned out to be Jake Forrester."

He had liked her before he found out about her dad? That was news to Star. Curious, she asked, "When did you think you might like me?"

"When you were staring at me instead of listening to Ms. Henry when she was scheduling the team picture."

Blushing, she felt heat rising all the way to , her eyebrows. "Was I that obvious?"

Rick's right hand curved around the back of her neck. It gave her goose bumps on her arms and she shivered.

He took a deep breath and asked hopefully, "Have we settled the thing about your father?"

Star realized that she had to face the big question. Did she really believe he had used her? Or did he like her for herself? The evidence had seemed so clear when she wanted to think that she had been nothing more than a convenient way for him to meet the band. But evidence can be misleading, Star argued with herself. When she didn't answer him, he pressed his fingers gently on her neck.

Suddenly the answer was obvious. She had missed him too much to be away from him any longer.

"Yes," Star said smiling shyly at Rick.

Feeling the happiest she had in a while, Star took his hand and they started walking again. His crooked grin made her curious. "What are you thinking?"

"I have a confession to make." Star tensed for a moment, but his relaxed manner told her not to worry. He explained, "I have to admit I was relieved when you didn't make the squad."

Star came to a stop, and her mouth fell open in dismay. "Relieved! How can you say that? I was cheated out of a spot I earned!"

"I didn't mean I was glad how it happened," he said quickly. "I still think they played the lowest trick on earth on you."

She narrowed her eyes in the direction of the kissing booth. He was right about that.

Rick's hand slipped under her chin and he gently tipped her head back so he could see her face. "I would have lost you permanently if you'd made the squad."

"I wouldn't have let that happen," she whispered, softly touching his cheek. It felt so good to be with him again. And things would be even better between them now with all the doubts and misunderstandings behind them.

"But you couldn't have stopped it," he told her. "I wouldn't have been a proper boyfriend for a cheerleader."

"Why not?" she asked, although she really knew the answer.

"I'm a yearbook editor who spends half his time with a camera around his neck." She couldn't help smiling when she remembered that Cyndi had once described him in a similar way. He caught her eye. "You've heard this before, haven't you?"

"I guess so." Star looked away, embarrassed that he knew she had listened to garbage like that.

"So here we are—two rejects from Cyndi's beautiful social club." He gazed over Star's head and laughed. "Speaking of Cyndi, no one's in line at the kissing booth, and she's on duty!" Grabbing her hand, Rick started to pull her in that direction.

"Forget it." Star tugged him in the opposite way. "I see something more interesting."

He agreed with her when he spied Mike Nelson sitting on the ledge of the dunk tank. "Let me knock him down for you."

"If you don't mind," she said, "I'd like to do it myself."

Rick paid the dollar for her and she took the two balls. Mike laughed and pretended he was frightened when he saw who was next in line, but she didn't pay any attention. Flexing her upper arm muscles, which were strong from years of swimming, she took aim. Her first pitch smashed the target directly in the center and Mike Nelson plunged into the water.

"I hope it's cold!" she exclaimed to Rick, enjoying her victory.

"Raffle time," they heard the yearbook editor call from the platform at the far end of the commons. Most of the people at the carnival crowded in that direction. Star noticed, however, that the cheerleaders huddled at their own booth while Cyndi glared.

Star and Rick managed to get fairly close to the platform. To Star's surprise, Rick dug into his pocket and pulled out nearly two dozen tickets. *What did he want so badly that he had bought so many chances?* She was convinced it was the television until she saw a complete set of Blue Street Fog albums. Star leaned forward to get a better look, and noticed the signatures of all three band members on the record jackets.

"Where did you get those albums?" she asked, astonished. "You can't find most of those records anymore." The only place she had seen some of them was in her basement.

"Your dad donated them," he said proudly.

"Did you happen to ask my dad for them the day BSF was on 'Twin Cities Happenings'?" She would really feel terrible if he had been working on the raffle when she thought he was at her house trying to get in good with her dad.

"Actually, I was picking them up. I'd called him before and asked if the band would like to donate anything. He left a message with my mom that I should stop by your house that day. I don't know which thing was more surprising, when he gave me the albums or when he asked me to watch the show with him!" His amazement was still obvious.

How could she have thought he had plotted to spend that time with her dad? "If you wanted the records so badly, why did you put them in the raffle? You could have kept them."

"I couldn't have done that!" He actually seemed shocked by the suggestion. "Besides, I don't want them. I didn't buy all these tickets hoping to win albums."

She glanced up quickly when he said that, but he wouldn't look her in the eye. Star knew he was keeping something from her but decided not to make a big deal about it. She knew he must have a reason.

"And now, who will take home this autographed set of Blue Street Fog albums?" The yearbook editor looked directly at Rick. "I know a few people who *really* want this prize. Every song BSF has ever recorded is in this collection."

Rick's hands were shaking when the editor started calling out the number. "A—one—six—seven—nine—two"

Star watched as Rick flipped through his stack. He did a double take on one ticket. He glanced at her, then glared at the piece of paper, and then he looked at her out of the corner of his eye. She craned her neck to read the number just before he sighed deeply and fanned through the rest of his tickets.

A16792! She had seen the number on the ticket he had stopped to study. He had it! Rick had the winning ticket! So why was he checking all his other numbers and shaking his head? He must not have realized he had the right one.

"You have it, Rick," she told him excitedly. "It's in the middle of your stack."

He closed his fist around his tickets. "No, I don't have it. You must have read one of them wrong."

"This is the last call for the albums. Who has A one-six-seven-nine-two?" the yearbook editor asked from the platform.

"I know you've got it." She wrestled the tickets out of his hand and pulled the winning number from the center of the stack. "Here it is! Look Rick!"

He took the ticket from her, and Star assumed he would wave it in the air and claim his prize. Nothing could have surprised her more than watching him rip the piece of paper into tiny pieces.

She took his arm and led him away as the editor called out another number for the same prize. "Why did you do that? You had the winning ticket."

"I know." His voice sounded casual, but the twitching muscle in his jaw told her he wasn't very happy.

"Don't tell me you bought all those tickets for anything else. I saw your hands shaking. I know you wanted the records."

He raised his arms in surrender. "Okay, I did want the albums. I bought the tickets yesterday—before I knew what would happen between us tonight."

"You're not making any sense." She reached out and touched his forehead. "Are you all right? You're not sick are you? I can't believe you just forfeited a collection of BSF records."

He took her wrist in his hand and moved it away from his face. "Don't worry. I'm not sick. Sure, I wanted the records, but I don't want them enough to risk losing you."

Star had no clue to what he was telling her. "Why would you lose me if you accepted the albums as your prize?"

His hand slipped from her wrist to her hand, and his fingers laced through hers. "I know you're worried that I'm more interested in Blue Street Fog than in you. We've just gotten back together tonight, and I don't want to ruin it. I didn't think you'd be very pleased to find out that I would do nearly anything to have that record collection."

She squeezed his hand to let him know she understood the sacrifice he had made. "I don't mind that you're a BSF fan. You've never imposed on my family or anything. All that taking advantage stuff was in my head. I can live with your feelings about BSF."

"You mean I could have taken the albums?" He slammed an open palm against his forehead.

Now that she knew Rick liked her for herself, she wanted to do something to make him feel better. It looked as if her wish for a boyfriend was back on track, and it seemed only fair one of *his* dreams should come true.

"What would you say, Rick Walsh, if I got you an autographed set of albums?"

He stared at her in surprise. "You don't mind that I want that collection more than *almost* anything else in the world?" She shook her head, and a happy grin started to curve across his face before he hurried to say, "You know that you're one of the only things I want more than the records. But could you really get them for me?"

She stood on tiptoe and put her lips against his to silence him. As soon as she caught her breath, she answered his question. "Of course I can get the records. After all, I'm Starshine Forrester. I've got connections."

Look Out Michael J. Fox, Here Comes Kirk Cameron!

Star of ABC-TV's hit series *Growing Pains*, Kirk Cameron is the hottest teen star in the country, receiving over 11,000 fan letters a month! Read the inside scoop about his early years as a child actor and what his life is like today at the top. You'll meet the real Kirk Cameron—on and off the screen!

* 24 pages of photographs!
* Interviews with Kurt Russell, Alan Thicke, Joanna Kerns and many more!
* Kirk's vital statistics—and how he stays in such great shape by working out with friends like Jason Bateman and Ricky Schroeder
* Kirk's innermost thoughts and feelings!
  "I've always been comfortable playing Mike . . . he's pretty close to the way I am."
  "I like all girls . . . the color of a girl's hair and the way she dresses don't matter at all."

Not to be missed!

☐ 27135 KIRK CAMERON: DREAM GUY $2.50

Prices and availability subject to change without notice.

STARFIRE

More good STARFIRE books for teenagers —from Bantam Books

☐ **GENTLEHANDS**   25773/$2.50
by M. E. Kerr
When a dark secret in his family's past is suddenly revealed, Buddy finds out that his Grandfather is the notorious Nazi war criminal, Gentlehands. By the author of *Dinky Hocker Shoots Smack* and *Little, Little*.

☐ **WITH A FACE LIKE MINE,**   13921/$2.25
YOU SETTLE FOR PERSONALITY
by Sharon L. Berman
Thirteen-year-old Raina-Ann is absolutely filled with envy when she meets beautiful and sophisticated Arielle. But as their friendship grows, so too does Raina-Ann's self-image.

☐ **WINNING**   25031/$2.50
by Robin Brancato
When a disastrous football injury puts Garry Madden in a wheelchair forever, it takes everything he's got, plus a little help from a friend, to handle the changes in his life and come up a winner.

☐ **HARRY AND HORTENSE**   25175/$2.95
AT HORMONE HIGH
by Paul Zindel
Harry and Hortense, students at chaotic Hormone High, don't know if Jason "Icarus" Rohr is the hero they've been waiting for—or a total madman. But from the very first it's clear that knowing Jason will change their lives forever. By the author of *The Pigman* and *My Darling, My Hamburger*.

☐ **ALL TOGETHER NOW**   26845/$2.75
by Sue Ellen Bridges

Casey had never lied before, at least not a big lie. But to
save her friendship with Dwayne, she was ready to do
anything. Even if it meant keeping a secret that would
last the whole summer long. By the author of *Home
Before Dark* and *Notes For Another Life.*

Prices and availability subject to change without notice.

Special Offer
Buy a Bantam Book
for only 50¢.

Now you can order the exciting books you've been wanting to read straight from Bantam's latest catalog of hundreds of titles. *And* this special offer gives you the opportunity to purchase a Bantam book for only 50¢. Here's how:

By ordering any five books at the regular price per order, you can also choose any other single book listed (up to a $5.95 value) for only 50¢. Some restrictions do apply, so for further details send for Bantam's catalog of titles today.

Just send us your name and address and we'll send you Bantam Book's SHOP AT HOME CATALOG!